both know something is going on ween us."

d glanced around and raked a nervous hand ugh his hair. "This isn't the place to have this ssion."

"No denial?" A grin tugged at Beth's mouth. "Well, that's progress."

"Don't get any ideas." He pressed the remote and unlocked the car doors.

"Too late." She laughed when he rolled his gaze heavenward, and reached for her door handle. And then he muttered something about the impulsiveness of youth. She stopped, thought a moment.

Impulsive, huh? She'd show him impulsive.

She opened the door, flung her purse onto the passenger seat, and then before he could climb in, went around the hood and threw her arms around his neck. He stumbled back in surprise, his hands going to her waist.

She smiled up at his shocked face. "How's this for impulsive?" And she kissed him.

Dear Reader,

What better way to celebrate June, a month of courtship and romance, than with four new spectacular books from Harlequin American Romance?

First, the always wonderful Mindy Neff inaugurates Harlequin American Romance's new three-book continuity series, BRIDES OF THE DESERT ROSE, which is a follow-up to the bestselling TEXAS SHEIKHS series. *In the Enemy's Embrace* is a sexy rivals-become-lovers story you won't want to miss.

When a handsome aristocrat finds an abandoned newborn, he turns to a beautiful doctor to save the child's life. Will the adorable infant bond their hearts together and make them the perfect family? Find out in *A Baby for Lord Roderick* by Emily Dalton. Next, in *To Love an Older Man* by Debbi Rawlins, a dashing attorney vows to deny his attraction to the pregnant woman in need of his help. With love and affection, can the expectant beauty change the older man's mind? Sharon Swan launches her delightful continuing series WELCOME TO HARMONY with *Home-Grown Husband*, which features a single-mom gardener who looks to her mysterious and sexy new neighbor to spice up her life with some much-needed excitement and romance.

This month, and every month, come home to Harlequin American Romance—and enjoy!

Best,

Melissa Jeglinski
Associate Senior Editor
Harlequin American Romance

TO LOVE
AN OLDER MAN
Debbi Rawlins

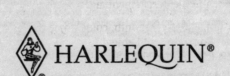

HARLEQUIN®

TORONTO • NEW YORK • LONDON
AMSTERDAM • PARIS • SYDNEY • HAMBURG
STOCKHOLM • ATHENS • TOKYO • MILAN • MADRID
PRAGUE • WARSAW • BUDAPEST • AUCKLAND

This is for Bernadette, my partner in crime.
I'm still waiting for you to write the next chapter.

ISBN 0-373-16927-2

TO LOVE AN OLDER MAN

Copyright © 2002 by Debbi Quattrone.

ABOUT THE AUTHOR

Debbi Rawlins currently resides with her husband in Las Vegas, Nevada. A native of Hawaii, she married on Maui and has since lived in Cincinnati, Chicago, Tulsa, Houston, Detroit and Durham, N.C., during the past twenty years. Now that she's had enough of the gypsy life, it'll take a crane, a bulldozer and a forklift to get her out of her new home. Good thing she doesn't like to gamble. Except maybe on romance.

Books by Debbi Rawlins

HARLEQUIN AMERICAN ROMANCE

HARLEQUIN INTRIGUE

Don't miss any of our special offers. Write to us at the following address for information on our newest releases.

Harlequin Reader Service
U.S.: 3010 Walden Ave., P.O. Box 1325, Buffalo, NY 14269
Canadian: P.O. Box 609, Fort Erie, Ont. L2A 5X3

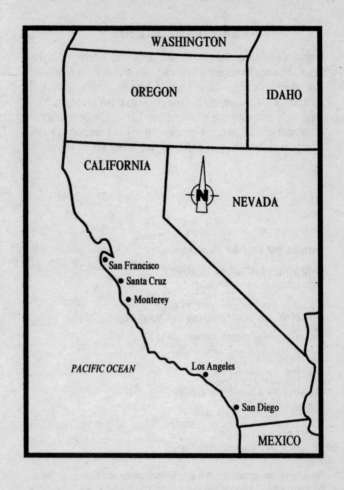

Chapter One

"Hey, Boss, it's eight-thirty. Aren't you ready to pack it up for the night?"

David Elliot Matthews looked up from his day planner at one of the firm's younger lawyers poking his blond head in David's office. "What are you still doing here?"

Todd shrugged. "Jason and I have the Sandburg's Metal fraud trial coming up next week. We're trying to get a head start on the case."

"Any problems?"

"No. Everything is under control," Todd said quickly, tugging at his loosened tie. "We just want to be prepared."

David suppressed a smile. They were young, only two years out of law school, and eager to make a good impression. As soon as he set foot in his private elevator, they'd head for Houlihan's bar on the first floor.

Fourteen years had passed since he graduated from law school himself, but he remembered those days when Houlihan's had just opened. His father had been head of the firm then, and found no amusement in the fact that his only son would rather party than practice law.

David Sr.'s first heart attack had been a sobering wake-up call for David. The second fatal attack changed David's life forever.

"Why don't you two go home? I'm headed out myself in a minute." His gaze drew to his day planner. Appointments filled page after page. He couldn't remember when he'd been able to eat a quiet lunch at his desk. Even the noon hours were blocked for meetings with the mayor, the chairperson of one charity or another, or perspective clients.

They always ate at Star Bistro or the St. Francis hotel. Damn if he could recall what a Big Mac tasted like.

"Yeah, we'll be wrapping it up soon." He glanced at his watch. "Have a good one."

"See you tomorrow." David had already transferred his gaze to his day planner. Only five appointments tomorrow. Maybe he'd have time to get on the treadmill for an hour.

He got up and stretched, and then picked his suit jacket up off the valet. Pausing a moment, he stared out at the lights across Fisherman's Wharf. San Francisco was his favorite city in the world.

Paris was beautiful in the spring and Athens possessed a certain magical quality at night. But there was no place like San Francisco for David. Not just because he'd grown up here. In fact, there were times when the prominent Matthews name made the city a difficult place to live, especially during his rebellious youth.

He shrugged on his jacket and watched the fog roll in. Another ten minutes and the glittering lights and the moon's reflection on the water would be shrouded with the thick damp haze. He didn't mind. There was something comforting and peaceful about the fog.

David grabbed his briefcase and a bottle of Evian from the wet bar for the ride home. His private elevator waited, and while he rode to the garage, he mentally ticked off the three briefs he had to review tonight. By tomorrow morning he had to…

The day planner—he'd left it on his desk.

Dammit.

His reserved parking stall was just outside the elevator doors and he pressed the button to unlock his car and then threw his briefcase onto the passenger seat. He hesitated, trying to decide how badly he needed the day planner.

Shaking his head, he locked the car doors again and then took the elevator back up.

He'd left his office door open for the cleaning crew and the light from the corridor was enough for him to get to his desk without breaking his neck. The day planner was still open right where he'd left it. He picked it up and then straightened his desk blotter when he heard a loud angry voice.

He stopped and listened. It wasn't Todd or Jason…David figured they'd left the moment they heard his elevator earlier. But as far as he knew, no one else was here.

Concerned, he moved closer to the door. He recognized the voice. Tom Snyder was their newest hire, a young lawyer only a year out of law school. Who the hell could he be talking to in that harsh tone? The guy was usually so well mannered.

David angled himself to get a better view. They were standing just outside Tom's door, Snyder and a young woman. Although David got only a shot of her profile, she looked barely out of her teens, her dark blond hair pulled back into a ponytail, her rumpled coat a size too big. With a trembling hand, she pushed stray tendrils of hair away from her flushed face.

"I don't want you here, Beth." Tom glared at the woman, his face darkened with rage. "Go back to Rock Falls."

"You know I can't do that," she said in a small defeated voice.

"I'll give you bus fare, but nothing more."

She wrapped her arms around herself. "You act as though I'm asking for a handout. It's my money, Tommy. You said you needed it for us, that once you had the right clothes and car and your career took off we could get married and I could go back to school."

"But you ruined it, didn't you? I told you I didn't want any kids tying me down. But you got yourself knocked up."

"You know it was an accident." She visibly swallowed but lifted her chin. "Besides, I seem to remember your participation."

Tom cursed viciously. "Go back to Idaho."

"Believe me, I don't want to stay here. Not with you." She shook her head. "You've changed, Tommy. I don't even know you anymore."

"And you haven't. You're still the idealistic little

girl who thinks all is right with the world as long as your apple pie wins the blue ribbon.''

She flinched. ''Please give me some of the money, Tommy. Just enough to go get set up somewhere. I don't care about the rest. You don't have to pay me back. You'll never have to see the baby or me again.''

David let out a breath, tamping down his growing anger. This was none of his business. He had no right eavesdropping. He never interfered in his employees' personal lives. He wouldn't start now, even though he'd like nothing better than to plant his fist in the middle of Snyder's arrogant face.

He had to leave. The feelings stirred inside him weren't about the young woman's plight as much as they were about David's own tumultuous youth, about the grave mistake he'd made almost twenty years ago.

''Did I say I'd pay you back?'' Tom asked, drawing David's attention back to the drama outside his office. ''I thought the money was a gift.''

''Tommy, please, I don't have anywhere to go tonight. Even if you don't care about me, you can't let our baby suffer.''

''Use your credit card.''

''You've maxed it out.''

''So this is my fault again.'' Tom swore and paced the corridor. ''I don't have any money. I don't get paid for another week. Can't you get an advance from your job?''

''You got me fired, remember?''

He stopped and glared, his face distorted with fury. ''Dammit, Beth, can't you accept responsibility for anything?''

Her mouth dropped open. She started to speak but then pressed her lips together and sadly shook her head.

"Go back to Idaho where big brother will make everything all right." Tom sneered. "Back to the farm where you belong."

"This isn't fair," she said, clutching her fists. "I'm only asking for what's mine."

"Life isn't fair. Haven't you figured that out yet?" He glanced at his watch. "Now I suggest you get out of here, which is what I'm about to do. I'd hate to have to call security."

David stepped back. The woman didn't appear to be in danger, which meant David had no business interfering. Making certain he had his day planner, he got in the elevator and headed for the garage.

He didn't know Tom Snyder well. Most of their interaction had occurred during the interviewing process, but he knew enough about the young man to be shocked by his behavior. David wasn't keen on having anyone of that ilk working for his firm. He had every intention of keeping a close eye on the guy. If he stepped out of line once, he was gone. Legally that was about the best he could do for now.

But that wasn't what weighed on David's mind. He couldn't erase the image of the young woman, her shoulders slumped in defeat, her trembling hands unconsciously rubbing her belly, which still appeared rather flat. Or maybe it was a trick of the oversized coat.

He wondered if she truly had no money. If not, where would she go tonight? Would she get anything to eat?

Not his concern, he reminded himself. The city had plenty of shelters and social services to assist her. Maybe Tom had even relented and put her up for the night.

Yeah, right.

The elevator reached the garage and the doors opened. David cursed to himself. He hesitated a second, staring at the Jaguar, longing for the relaxing ride home, and then pressed the button to return to the top floor.

No doubt he'd regret what he was about to do. But if he didn't assure himself the woman was all right, he'd regret that, too. Hopefully, they'd both be gone and he wouldn't have to get involved.

Not a sound came from the corridor as he left the elevator. He paused at his office door and listened. Only silence. He stepped out into the hall and immediately saw her. No sign of Tom—just the young woman sitting in a crumpled heap near the public elevator, her head bowed, her long blond hair falling forward and hiding her face.

"Excuse me?" David said, and her head shot up, her big blue eyes startled and wary. "Can I help you?"

"No." She pushed out of the chair. "Thank you. I was just waiting for the elevator."

She was young, really young, just as he'd thought. He gave her a reassuring smile. "Are you here to see someone?"

She bit her lower lip, probably to keep it from quivering, and then pressed the elevator button. "I know it's late. I promise I'll leave the building as soon as the elevator gets here."

A swift and fierce hatred for Tom Snyder gripped

David. How could the guy have treated this young woman so callously? She was obviously a wreck, and still she tried to protect him. She could have announced why she was here, embarrass Tom. But she hadn't.

"I'm not concerned about you leaving the building but I'd like to know where you're going."

She stared in surprise. "Why?"

He nodded at the small bag on the floor beside her. "Is that yours?"

"Yes," she mumbled and bent to pick it up. She looked unsteady as she straightened and he reached for her arm. She jerked away, fear darkening her blue eyes.

"I'm sorry." He withdrew his hand. What the hell was he doing getting involved? Put him in a courtroom and he could make judges weep. Here, he was no better than a bull in a china shop. "I didn't mean to frighten you."

She shrunk against the wall, her gaze darting down the corridor. Looking as though she wanted to make a run for it.

"I better introduce myself," he said quickly. "I'm David Matthews." Recognition registered in her face, but he added, "I own this firm."

She blinked and then her eyes narrowed as she drew back.

He reached into his pocket and withdrew his wallet. "See?" He showed her his driver's license, and impulsively placed his thumb over his birth date.

She wrinkled her nose. "I believed you. It's just that you're not that old."

"Pardon me?"

She quickly averted her eyes, her cheeks flushing a deep pink, and she jabbed at the elevator button again.

"At this time of night security shuts down all but one elevator. It's going to be a while."

She said nothing, only stared down at her battered pink tennis shoes.

"Beth?"

Her gaze flew back to him. "How do you know my name?"

"I heard you and Tom arguing." He hated that he made her uncomfortable, had put humiliation in her face, but there was no getting around it. "Where are you staying tonight?"

She briefly closed her eyes and swayed slightly. He squashed the urge to steady her. "Please, I didn't mean to cause any trouble."

"You haven't. From what I heard, Tom was being…" *A total ass.* "…less than honorable. Is he still here?"

Beth shook her head, wishing the darn elevator doors would open and swallow her up. She should never have come here. What had she hoped to accomplish? Tommy wasn't going to budge. All she'd done was totally humiliate herself in front of a stranger.

"I'll be fine, really. Thank you for asking." She turned her back on his dark penetrating eyes, and faced the elevator.

"Beth? May I call you that?" he asked, and she jumped when he touched her arm.

"Sure." She shrugged, and shifted away. His voice was gentle, concerned, and she struggled to hold herself together.

"I know you must be embarrassed and a little frightened." He paused when she refused to acknowledge him. "I know I would be in your shoes. But you do have to think about the baby."

A sob caught in her throat. She couldn't speak even if she wanted to. Not that she had anything to say. He was right, but she felt so darn helpless.

"I have a large house with three guest rooms. You're welcome to stay the night."

Of course she couldn't accept his offer but she still couldn't speak either. If she did, she feared the flood-gates would open.

He pushed a rough hand through his short dark hair, and she realized he wasn't as calm as he seemed. "I assure you this offer is on the up-and-up. My mother has a suite of rooms on the third floor. Our house-keeper has an apartment over the garage."

Beth relaxed a little. He was being awfully kind. But surely she'd find a shelter that could take her in for the night. She opened her mouth to refuse, but before she could say a word, her stomach rumbled. She groaned at the loud, obnoxious sound, and mut-tered, "Must be the baby."

He smiled. "Let the little guy know I have a fully stocked kitchen."

"It might be a girl."

"Of course."

"It's too early. I haven't found out yet." Oh, God, she was babbling.

He didn't seem put off, but smiled again. "Just for tonight. Tomorrow you'll be better rested, the baby's belly will be full and you can decide what you want to do."

She shook her head. "Thank you, but—"

"Beth, you have your baby to think about." His

words were quiet, gentle but they cut through her like a butcher's knife.

She wrapped her arms around herself, recalling the cold damp fog that had started to roll in an hour ago. Foolishly she'd hoped she'd have a nice warm room by now. She sighed and rubbed the slight swell of her tummy. Mr. Matthews was right. This wasn't only about her anymore. She had the baby to worry about.

Still, it was difficult to bring herself to accept charity. It was a new experience. Even after her parents had died ten years ago, and her brother took charge of both her and the farm, she'd always been self-sufficient.

But she hadn't had a baby to worry about, she reminded herself. She took a deep breath. "Thank you, Mr. Matthews. We—I'll accept your kind offer. On one condition."

His left brow went up.

"I pay you back when I'm able." She knew he meant nothing by it, but his patronizing expression annoyed her. "That's how it has to be."

His forehead creased in thought and he pursed his lips. They were nice lips, not too thin, not too full. Perfect, really. "The thing is, I've got to pay my mortgage whether you stay tonight or not."

She saw the amused glint in his eyes, and folded her arms across her chest and sat down on the upholstered bench between the elevator doors. Fine. If she had to wait all night for the darn elevator at least she'd be warm and dry.

A short startled laugh made her look up. He put on a straight face, but a smile lurked at the corners of his mouth. "Come on, Beth." He offered her a hand. "Let's discuss it in the car."

Her stomach growled again. She tried sucking it in to stop the noise. No luck. "All right, Mr. Matthews, but you know my terms."

He took the bag from her hand. "I have a condition, as well. Call me David. I may be old enough to be your father but—"

"You are not. I'm twenty-five." She'd fudged only a little. Her birthday was in a month.

He looked surprised.

She studied the faint smile lines at the corners of his eyes. "How old are you?"

He frowned and cleared his throat. "Let's get on the road. I'll call Ida to keep dinner warm."

"Don't let her go to any trouble." She didn't understand why he left the elevator and headed in the opposite direction, but she followed him through double mahogany doors.

"Don't worry. She's going to love fussing over you," he said over his shoulder. "So will my mother."

Beth slowed down as soon as she realized she was in his office. Although it didn't look like any office she'd ever seen. The room was massive, two sides of it was all windows overlooking the city lights. A wet bar with gold-framed mirrors occupied one corner, an elaborate stereo system the other.

One entire wall was a floor-to-ceiling bookshelf filled with texts. They weren't all law books either. She spotted a couple of current works of fiction she'd just read herself.

A treadmill was off to the side, hidden behind an Oriental screen. A television and two plump sofas and a pair of leather armchairs were arranged in a surprisingly cozy setting. Her gaze drew to his large desk, but settled on him when she realized he was staring at her.

She gave him a small smile. "Wow! This is some office."

His gaze flickered across the room and he frowned slightly. "Yes, I suppose it is."

Behind him came a low beep. She gaped at the polished brown oak door sliding open. "You have your own private elevator?"

One side of his mouth lifted. "So it seems. Are you coming?"

He motioned her past him and she scurried inside, and then waited for him to join her. He pressed the garage button and then silently faced the door for their ride down.

Beth tried not to be obvious as she eyed his clean-shaven jaw. At this late hour, she didn't know how he could have no stubble...unless he'd shaved in the afternoon again. His hair was perfectly cut, a dark rich brown with no sign of gray. He wasn't nearly as old or stern as Tommy had said.

He was obviously a very nice man to take in a total stranger like this. Back in Rock Falls, that sort of kindness was taken for granted, but she hadn't encountered anything like it in the city yet. That it was Tommy's boss who'd come to her rescue filled her with a perverse pleasure that Grandma Anderson would have threatened to take a switch to her for.

Beth smiled. Not that Grand had ever laid a hand, or switch, on her. But Grand was such a tiny and good-hearted woman, Beth figured she needed the bluff to keep her grandkids in line. Especially Junior and his horrendous temper.

The sudden thought of her brother made her feel a

little queasy and she pressed a hand to her stomach. Junior was the best brother a girl could ever have. He was supportive, caring and protective. Too protective. He never had liked Tommy to begin with…if Junior ever found out what he'd done…

"Are you all right?"

Beth looked up. David's concerned gaze lifted from the hand at her tummy to meet her eyes. They were nice eyes, dark but with interesting flecks of gold. "Fine. Really. I was just thinking about…stuff."

"Ah." He gave an understanding nod. "Maybe you should wait until you've had something to eat and had a good night's rest before you think about any more…stuff."

She started to respond but the elevator door opened, and he held it back for her. She hesitated, but couldn't form the right words quickly enough and stepped out instead. He indicated a dark green Jaguar several feet away, and then pressed something in his hand that produced a clicking noise. The door locks, she realized, when he overtook her and opened the passenger door.

A black leather briefcase sat on the seat, but he carefully placed it in the back, along with her bag, and then continued to hold the door for her while she slid inside. He ducked and she jumped, feeling foolish when she realized he only wanted to make sure her coat didn't get caught in the door.

She was fairly sure he noticed her edginess but he didn't say anything. He went around the hood of the car and climbed in behind the wheel and reversed out of the stall without a word. After he made a call on his cell phone, he pressed a button and soft classical music filled the car.

They didn't say anything for the next fifteen minutes. He drove and she stared out the window at the thickening fog, grateful that she and the baby had a warm dry place to stay for the night. But what would she do tomorrow night? And the night after that? It wasn't easy looking for a job while pregnant. She didn't show much yet but that would probably change in a month. Of course she could keep doing temp work but the pay was low and barely covered a place to live.

"Hey, you aren't thinking about stuff again, are you?"

She turned away from the window and looked at him. He took his eyes away from the road long enough to give her a smile. It was kind and reassuring, but a little patronizing, too, and she couldn't hold back any longer.

"Mr., uh, David, I really appreciate what you're doing for me. But I'm not a child. Don't treat me like one."

Chapter Two

David couldn't wait to unload her on his mother. Had he really been treating Beth like a child? What had he said? He'd only advised her not to worry, not when she was tired and hungry. Anyway, she was young. Twenty-five was still...

Hell, he'd graduated from law school at twenty-five and if anyone had so much as implied that he wasn't a fully capable adult he would've had a few choice words for them. It didn't matter that he'd still been riding his motorcycle without a helmet or that he always forgot to balance his checkbook, or that he'd let his bills stack up for two months at a time even though he'd had plenty of money in his account.

Part of it was that Beth looked so young with her big blue eyes and scattering of freckles across her nose. She was short, probably not even five-two and her long hair hung past her shoulders in no particular style, the way girls used to wear it back in high school.

He cursed to himself. High school. Amazing he could remember that far back. It seemed like a century ago.

"You don't live in the city?" Beth asked as they

turned onto the bridge, her eyes widening on the arched lights of the Golden Gate.

"No, Sausalito."

"I've never been there."

He glanced at her in surprise. "How long have you been living in San Francisco?"

"Almost a year. But Tommy and I always seemed to be working so we didn't go out much."

Amazing how calmly she could speak of the jerk, when he himself wanted to punch the guy's lights out. "What do you do?"

"I *was* a secretary." She sighed. "But I got fired. I also worked as a waitress three evenings a week, but…" She turned to the window again, her shoulders sagging. "It didn't work out."

No doubt Tom had a hand in getting her fired at that, as well. But she still said nothing negative about him, for which David didn't know if he should admire her or shake her. Of course, he reminded himself, it was none of his business.

She was none of his business. Only one night's lodging. That's all he'd offered her. As she'd pointedly informed him, she was not a child. She could take care of herself, even though she looked as if she were fifteen.

He knew what was really bothering him. His birthday was coming up next month. The big one. And his mother had some awful notion that she should have a huge party for him. As if turning forty was something to celebrate.

Well, there wouldn't be any damn party, even if he had to take off to Hawaii for the weekend. He glanced over at Beth, who'd turned back to staring out the window. Maybe she was just the distraction his mother needed.

He slowed as they approached the security gate at the bottom of his driveway. Beth gasped when he started to punch in the code to let them in, and he darted her a look.

"You live here?" Her eyes were wide with surprise, her lips curved.

He followed her gaze toward the house, or at least what could be seen of it through the trees and darkness. There were a lot of lights on but he wasn't sure what had interested her. "This is home, all right."

"It's huge, and there are so many lights and windows. Can you see the ocean from there?"

"It's built into the hill but we have a pretty good view of the bay from most rooms." He finished putting in the code and watched the gate slowly swing open.

As he drove up the winding driveway his gaze drew to the house. He'd had it built as high on the hill as possible for maximum view and privacy with more windows than was probably prudent. He had to admit, the place did look quite impressive with all the lights blazing through the trees. It had been a long time since he'd noticed or appreciated its simple beauty.

"Gosh, this is incredible." Beth continued to stare, wide-eyed as they rounded a curve into a clearing before the garden crawled up the slope to the house. "Keeping this place in shape must take all your weekends."

David laughed, but then realized she was serious when she darted him an odd look.

She made a face. "That was silly of me. Of course you have someone to help you with all this."

Help? He cleared his throat. Not only had he never set foot in the garden, he couldn't tell one flower from another. He hit the garage-door opener and impatiently edged the car in while the door lifted.

As soon as they got inside, Beth would be his mother's problem. She'd love every second of the fussing, and he could get to work. In his den. Alone. The thought held enormous appeal. Not that Beth was a bother but he liked routine, and having her beside him for the past half hour was anything but normal.

He parked, turned off the engine and unfastened his seat belt. Beth sat motionless. He glanced over. She was pale.

"What's wrong?"

She winced. "Nothing, really."

"Why are you holding your stomach?"

"It's nothing."

David hesitated, unsure what to do. Should he press her? Assume it really was nothing? Where the hell was his mother?

Beth laid a hand on his arm. "Don't worry. It's not the baby or anything. I'm just a little carsick."

Her touch was gentle, featherlight, yet it sparked an odd sensation in him. Quickly he shifted away and got out of the car. "I may have taken the curves too fast. I wish you'd said something."

"I'm sorry."

"No need to apologize. I didn't mean to—" He

shook his head and went around the car to open her door. First opportunity he got, he was going to fire Tom Snyder's ass. The guy had been such a jerk to the poor girl; she thought she had to apologize for getting sick.

She'd already opened her door and swung her legs out of the car by the time he got there. He stopped and stared at her shapely calves and slim ankles. She was short but all legs. Great legs.

Fortunately she was too busy trying to hold her stomach and lift herself out of the car to notice him staring. His reaction disgusted him. He had no business wondering what the rest of her looked like under that big coat. None whatsoever.

"Here." He offered her a hand.

"I'm okay, but if you'd get my bag I'd appreciate it." Her gaze warily slid up the stairs going to the kitchen door.

Hell, he'd forgotten about that. The garage had been built under the house and his mother sometimes complained the stairs were too steep.

He stood aside while she got out by herself but as they approached the stairs he took her elbow.

She didn't protest, but simply held the railing with one hand and her tummy with the other. He hoped she was right, and that her queasiness was a result of carsickness. That would pass within an hour.

"I'm really not such a wimp, you know," she said, a little breathless, as she looked over at him.

Her eyes were the clearest blue he'd ever seen and her skin was nearly flawless. Her face was still pale but some rest and a good meal would probably take care of that.

"Not for a moment have I thought of you as a wimp. Watch your step."

"Oops." She faltered, but he tightened his hold on her elbow and she leaned into him.

A subtle fragrance drifted up from her hair. Jasmine. Or maybe gardenia. He inhaled deeply. Definitely jasmine. "Okay?"

She nodded and straightened. "My coat's too big. I almost tripped on the hem." She looked up at him, her eyes so innocent and blue and something stirred inside him.

"We'll have to do something about that," he murmured, thrown off balance by the sudden urge he had to pick her up and carry her the rest of the way up the stairs.

"David?"

At his mother's voice, he looked up at the top of the stairs. She stood at the open door, a perplexed look on her face as her gaze slid between him and Beth.

He quelled the asinine impulse to release Beth. But they'd done nothing wrong. "Hi, Mother, I hope I'm not keeping you awake."

"Nonsense." She smiled at Beth, and then stepped back to hold the door open for them. "He didn't worry about keeping me awake forty years ago," she said, winking at Beth. "The little monster kept me in labor for thirty-two hours."

Beth darted a surprised look at him.

He glared at his mother. He wasn't forty yet.

"Mother, this is Beth—" He stopped when he realized he had no idea what Beth's last name was.

"Anderson."

"I'm Maude."

He breathed a sigh of relief as the women took over. Or more accurately, his mother had taken charge. She ushered Beth through the laundry room to the kitchen, sat her down and got her a glass of water. Ida was already in the kitchen, stirring something in a pot. It smelled like her homemade chicken soup. David hadn't had any in ages.

"Be a love and put Beth's bag in the blue guest room," his mother said, "and then come back down and have something to eat."

She gave him only a brief glance and then all her attention went back to Beth who looked a bit over-whelmed. David didn't bother telling her he'd had a late lunch and would have a snack later while he worked in his den. He seldom got home early enough to eat dinner at home. Anyway, she was already busy tending to Beth, looking more animated than he'd seen her in a long time.

He carried the bag to the first floor guest room, and then went to his own room upstairs to get out of his suit. At least two hours of work waited for him in his briefcase and…

His briefcase—he'd left it in the car.

Dammit.

He shrugged out of his coat, loosened and pulled off his tie, got rid of the gold cuff links. He hated the possibility of going through the kitchen and getting waylaid. Bad enough he'd lost an hour already, but he had no choice. He needed the briefs and his day planner.

David swore. He'd left his day planner on his desk again. He sat on the edge of his bed and pulled off his socks. God, he hated being thrown off his routine.

"NOW, BETH, anything you need, you feel free to ask." Mrs. Matthews set the cup of tea beside the glass of water she'd already filled twice, and Beth wanted to cry. "In fact, if you see it, don't ask, help yourself."

"You're being so kind," Beth murmured, overwhelmed with gratitude for the unexpected thoughtfulness these strangers showed her. "Please don't make a big fuss. I'm fine."

"Nonsense. We're not fussing. Are we, Ida?"

The housekeeper gave a dismissive snort as she ladled rich yellow broth into a bowl. Her round face had been wreathed in a welcoming smile from the minute Beth laid eyes on her. She was probably the same age as Mrs. Matthews, early sixties, Beth guessed. But as slim and tall as Mrs. Matthews was, Ida was short and plump. They made quite a pair in their contrasting red silk and gray chenille robes.

"It's been too long since David has brought a friend home," Mrs. Matthews put a carafe of coffee on the table, and then brought out cups. Not mugs, but real china cups and saucers.

"I'm not exactly a friend," Beth muttered, not sure what David had told them.

"Well, we're delighted to have you. Would you rather eat in the dining room?"

"This is fine." Beth watched Ida root through the refrigerator. "Please don't go to any more trouble."

She brought out what looked like a lemon meringue pie. Only one small piece was missing. "Trouble?" Ida grunted. "About time there's someone around here to eat my pastries. Those two take one little nibble and start worrying about their arteries."

Mrs. Matthews sighed and threw Ida a long-suffering look. "You put a pound of butter in everything you bake."

"Neither of my parents knew what an artery was and they both lived until ninety-six." Ida sniffed. "Mind you, they ate plenty of butter and cheese, too."

Beth laughed. The two women obviously shared a friendship beyond the employer-employee relationship.

Mrs. Matthews laughed, too. "Don't mind us. Ida and I go back more years than we care to admit."

"Quit talking and let the poor girl eat." Ida put two dessert plates on the table and then took a seat and picked up a knife.

"You're having another piece of pie?" Mrs. Matthews asked, as she sat across from Beth with a cup of black coffee.

"You mind your business, Maude." Ida smiled at Beth. "So, how do you know our David?"

Beth had just swallowed a mouthful of the chicken soup but she pretended to chew. The truth was pretty embarrassing, yet she didn't want to lie, either.

"And you tell me to mind my business?" Mrs. Matthews's perfectly arched brows went up. "Really, Ida, can't you let the young lady eat in peace?"

Color climbed all the way to Ida's salt-and-pepper hairline. "Of course. Eat." She motioned with her chin to Beth before digging into the large wedge of lemon meringue in front of her.

Beth quickly spooned up another portion of the delicious soup. She was hungry but also grateful there'd be no more questions. At least for now.

Mrs. Matthews looked exactly like Beth would have pictured her had she thought about it. Perfectly styled chestnut-colored hair, even at bedtime, perfect teeth, a perfect figure. Her nails were manicured and polished a subtle pink. She looked and smelled rich. Old money rich. Just like David.

Of course they were from old money, according to Tommy. Their family went back to the gold rush days when the Matthews name became a prominent San Francisco fixture. In the legal arena, their firm was number one, if she could believe Tommy. He seemed awfully impressed with that kind of social stuff these days, so she figured he ought to know.

What impressed Beth was the way Mrs. Matthews treated Ida. The woman was a polar opposite—on the frumpy side, her curly graying hair in need of a trim, her roughened hands looked like those of a farmer's wife.

"Are you ready for another bowl?" Ida asked, and to Beth's humiliation, she realized she'd practically inhaled her food.

"No, thank you. This was plenty."

Ida grunted as she got up and took Beth's empty bowl. "That was hardly enough to keep a bird alive."

"But I had two pieces of that great bread. Did you make it?"

Ida nodded, her face one big smile. "No store-bought baked goods in this house."

"She's determined to make me fat." Mrs. Matthews sipped her black coffee with a look of phony disdain.

"Don't mind her. She thinks three strawberries with a teaspoon of fat-free whipped cream is dessert."

Beth smiled. "Sorry, but nothing beats real whipped cream, or freshly churned butter. I haven't had either since I left the farm."

Both women stared at her. Ida spoke first as she set another bowl of soup in front of Beth. "You actually lived on a farm?"

Beth nodded, and silently cursed her big mouth. These people would think she was some kind of hick. She brought her napkin to her lips—a linen napkin, no common paper stuff here. That she'd momentarily been ashamed of her roots shamed her even more. First her parents, and then her brother provided her with a good home in Rock Falls. Better than good, it had been idyllic.

She lifted her chin. "Back in Rock Falls, Idaho. My family has owned it for five generations. We were all born right there in the master bedroom."

"My heavens." Mrs. Matthews set down her coffee cup, the china making a pleasant tinkling sound. "How long have you been here in the city?"

"A little over a year."

Mrs. Matthews's brows drew together in a sympathetic frown, and Beth's defenses soared. "How you must have hated to leave."

"I'll say." Ida placed another bowl of the steaming soup in front of Beth. "Why did you?"

She didn't know what to say. Not because of Tommy, but because she'd expected disdain, because she'd been prepared to defend her rural childhood.

She shrugged. "My brother works the farm now. He lives there with his wife and three kids."

"You two aren't grilling our guest, I hope."

David's voice had all three of them turning toward him.

He stood at the door, rolling back the sleeves of his blue oxford shirt, which he'd left unbuttoned at the top. He'd traded his suit pants for jeans and his black dress shoes for battered brown loafers, no socks. The casual look shaved ten years off him, and a totally inappropriate flutter in Beth's chest startled her.

She hiccupped.

Oh, God. Not now.

Mrs. Matthews turned to her. "Are you okay?"

Beth nodded, and hiccupped again.

Ida jumped up and went to the sink. "Hold your breath for ten seconds while you drink down this water," she said while she filled a glass. "It works every time."

"Nonsense. That's an old wives' tale." Mrs. Matthews waved a dismissive hand, but she said nothing more as Ida handed Beth the glass.

She hiccupped again, and then carefully avoided looking at David while she started to down the water. Slowly she counted to ten, and wondered if this evening could possibly get any more humiliating. Nerves hadn't caused a hiccupping fit for almost five years. Why now?

She set down the glass and everyone waited in mortifying silence to see if Ida's cure worked.

No more hiccups. She was afraid to so much as smile.

Ida planted her hands on her hips with a triumphant grin. "What did I tell you?"

Mrs. Matthews sighed. "I suppose we'll hear about this for the next two weeks."

"Indeed you would if I were going to be here."

David went to the refrigerator and opened it. "Where are you going to be?"

"On vacation. I'm going to Denver to see my grandbabies," Ida said, eyeing Mrs. Matthews who remained silent and apparently displeased, judging from her pinched expression.

"Good for you." David took out an apple. "I'm glad to see you take some time off."

"Nice someone's happy for me," Ida mumbled and got up and cleared the pie off the table. "Beth, can I get you anything else?"

Beth cleared her throat and prayed the hiccups were truly over. "No, thank you." She briefly glanced at David who was giving his mother some kind of silent warning. "You've both been very kind, but please don't let me keep you up."

David pulled a chair out and sat down. The two women looked at him in clear astonishment. "Mother, you and Ida go on to bed. I'll take care of Beth."

The women exchanged startled glances, their differences temporarily forgotten.

Beth experienced a jolt of surprise herself. She hadn't expected him to have anything else to do with her. He seemed more than happy to leave her to his mother's care earlier. Not that she blamed him. She was a stranger, an intruder into his private life.

"Thank you for helping out," he said. "Now, I'm sure there's something on television you're missing."

Ida tightened the belt of her robe. "I would like to put my feet up. Anything special you'd like for breakfast?"

Busy staring at David, Beth belatedly realized Ida was talking to her. "Uh, no, thanks. I'll be leaving early tomorrow morning."

Mrs. Matthews had stood and picked up her cup and saucer. But she stopped and frowned at Beth. "But I—"

"Good night, Mother."

She sighed and gave her son the eye. "I'd like to speak with you before you go to bed."

"I'll be in after I get Beth settled in her room."

The simple statement sounded so intimate goose bumps surfaced on Beth's arms. What the heck was wrong with her? Haywire hormones? Did that happen so soon into the pregnancy? She was woefully ignorant about such matters. At least if she were back in Rock Falls…

She put the brakes on. Going home was not an option. No sense in getting melancholy about it. She had to move forward, think about where she would stay, how she would support herself, get medical insurance…

The two older women had said good-night and were

leaving the kitchen before Beth realized how lost in thought she'd been. Quickly she called out a good-night, and then silence descended. She'd already finished her soup and a third slice of bread. If she didn't think she'd burst at the seams, she would've had another just for an excuse not to talk.

But there was a downside to the silence. More worries germinated and grew inside her exhausted brain. The small amount of money she had left in the bank would take her through one day. Hopefully she'd get a temp job tomorrow, but what if she couldn't?

"I should have warned you about those two," David finally said, his voice serious, but when she looked at him one side of his mouth was lifted. "I hope they weren't too nosy."

"Oh, no, they were incredibly kind." She swallowed around the sudden lump in her throat. "They made me feel so welcome. I—I—"

Oh, God, not now.

The tears came in buckets.

Chapter Three

Great. This was terrific. David set aside the apple and then wiped his hands on a napkin, trying not to notice how fragile she looked in that oversized coat she'd oddly refused to take off. Had he said something inflammatory? What was he supposed to do now? He could call his mother...

Nah, he wasn't that big a coward. Hell, he headed a multimillion-dollar law firm. He could handle this small problem. He cleared his throat, got her a box of tissues and then gave her several awkward pats on her back while he searched his helpless brain for something to say.

She dabbed at her eyes, blew her reddened nose. "I'm sorry," she said, reluctantly raising her watery blue eyes to him. "I have no idea where that came from."

He withdrew his hand. "You're probably just tired."

She sniffed and snuggled deeper into her coat as if for protection. "That's no excuse."

"Don't be so hard on yourself."

Her gaze came up, her eyes bright, and he thought she might start crying again.

"This is a tough time for you," he added quickly. "Uncertainty is difficult to face under the best circumstances and now you have a baby to consider."

"Thank you," she whispered, "for being so understanding. I'm really not such a wimp."

The sincere gratitude in her eyes got to him and he touched the tip of her nose. "I don't doubt that for a moment."

The rest of her face got as red as her nose. "You're treating me like a child again."

"What?"

"Don't deny it." A teasing smile started at the corners of her mouth. "But that's okay. I'm used to it. I look young for my age, plus my brother and his friends were so much older that they've always treated me like a kid."

"Is that why you won't go back to Idaho?"

Any trace of a smile vanished and she hunched her shoulders. "Not exactly."

"I'm prying. I apologize." He knew little about pregnancy but enough to understand that a woman's body and mood changed. And boy, did he just get a sample of it. If she started crying again it would be his fault.

"You have a right to know. After all, you've taken me in."

"Just for the night."

Embarrassment rose in her cheeks. "I understand. I'll be leaving first thing tomorrow morning."

"I didn't mean that. What I was trying to say in a

very bad way was that you don't owe me any explanations. My offer wasn't conditional.''

''I know.'' She sighed. ''My brother has a notoriously bad temper. If he finds out about Tommy taking my college money—'' She pressed her lips together, panic flickering in her eyes, as if she'd said too much. ''Anyway, Junior and his wife work the farm now. They have three children. There's really no room for me there.''

''And your parents?''

''They died when I was fifteen. Junior took over my guardianship.''

''He's your only sibling, I take it.''

She nodded. ''Even though he's twelve years older than me we're very close, but he wouldn't understand me getting pregnant. He never liked Tommy.'' She stared down at her hands. ''I guess Junior was right about him.''

''Nevertheless, surely your brother wouldn't turn you away.''

She looked up, her eyes troubled. ''Oh, no, of course not.'' She blinked, looked away. ''It's complicated.''

''And none of my business.''

She gave him a tiny apologetic smile. The discussion was closed. He respected that, and to reassure her, he laid a hand on her clasped ones. They were cold and fidgety, and she was so small his one hand covered them both.

Her eyes widened, slightly, just enough to spark an awareness in him that made his mouth go dry, his chest tighten. Trust…gratitude…were both there in her unguarded expression. He pulled away and raked a hand through his hair.

"I'm sure you're tired." He stood and disposed of his half-eaten apple. "Let me show you to your room."

She got to her feet, her gaze following him with a wariness that unsettled him. "Did I do something wrong?"

"Of course not. I just figured you wanted to rest."

She pushed back the sleeves of her coat. "I'm going to do the dishes first. Is the soap under the sink?"

David grunted. "You are not going to wash the dishes."

"I'm certainly not going to leave them." She brushed past him with her bread plate and bowl.

"We have a dishwasher." His gaze scanned the room. He knew they had one somewhere…. Ah, he spotted it to the right of the sink.

"I'm sure Ida has already run it for the night. It won't take me long to wash these up." She placed the dishes in the sink and turned on the water. Her coat sleeves slid back down and she pushed them up again.

David shut the water off, and when she turned to him he placed his hands on her shoulders. "You are not going to wash dishes. You are going to bed."

He'd expected her to comply but she surprised him by tilting her head back and narrowing her gaze. "Says who?"

The forgotten childhood taunt startled a laugh out of him. "Says me."

They stood staring at each other a moment, and then

a shy smile tugged at her lips and she moved back. "Really, I can wash up everything in no time."

He lowered his hands. She had such slim shoulders a peculiar protectiveness stirred inside him. "You're a guest in this house. If I let you so much as lift a finger, my mother and Ida will run me up a flagpole."

She made a face. "I'm not exactly a guest."

"I suggest you follow me, or you're on your own to find the guest room."

He headed out of the kitchen, hiding a smile when she scurried after him. Halfway across the dining room he heard her gasp and he made an abrupt about-face.

"Wow, this house is really something."

Her gaze swept the two-story white marble foyer with the crystal chandelier his mother had found in Rome. The living room was decorated in a simple but elegant contemporary style, the real focal point the city beyond the wide expanse of glass. San Francisco twinkled like a hundred-carat diamond.

David watched the wonder light her eyes and suffered a surprising pang of envy. He remembered how excited he'd been over the architectural plans, and how he used to stand on the hill before the house was built and just stare at the city below, waiting, anticipating.

Now it seemed all he did was work. Which reminded him...he still had to get his briefcase out of the car and start in on that brief....

"Your room is right down this hall," he said with more impatience than he'd intended.

"Sorry." She threw one final admiring look around and then hurried after him.

The bedroom was already made up. Ida kept it in

top shape for unexpected guests. He'd already put Beth's bag on the luggage rack near the closet. The tote was so light he wondered what she had in there. Clearly she had to have more clothes stashed somewhere.

"There's a bathroom behind the door to the left, the one on the right goes out onto a balcony. Let's see, there are hangers and an extra blanket in the closet, bottled water over in that small fridge in the corner."

She stood in the doorway, as if afraid to come all the way into the room.

He casually stepped back to give her space. "Can you think of anything else you might need?"

She shook her head, her eyes looking suspiciously bright again. Definitely his cue to leave.

"Okay, then, good night." He eased between her and the door.

"David?" She touched his arm, and when he stopped, she rose on tiptoes and kissed his cheek. "Thank you."

Her warm breath and subtle jasmine scent stirred more than friendly concern and panic surged in his chest. "No problem," he said with unintended gruffness, and then got the hell out of her room.

"GOOD MORNING." Ida was all smiles in a shocking pink dress and yellow apron, her curly graying hair less wild this morning. "You're just in time. I made another fresh pot of coffee."

Beth yawned, and covered her mouth in embarrassment. Bad enough she'd slept so late. Back on the farm she would have been up for over two hours already. "Good morning. Or should I say good afternoon?"

Ida handed her a cup. "Phooey. It's only nine."

Beth gave the carafe of rich brown brew a longing look. Caffeine wasn't good for the baby. But maybe there was a period early in the pregnancy that allowed one cup. She had no idea. There was so much to learn...

"Are you gonna stare it to death or drink it?" Ida picked up the carafe and held it above Beth's cup.

"Just half, please."

"There's only a measly fifty percent caffeine in this blend," Ida said, and filled Beth's cup to the brim. "Her Highness worries about too much of that, too."

"Mrs. Matthews?"

Ida chuckled. "Don't look so scandalized. I always call her that, and to her face, mind you. Have a seat."

Beth took the same chair she'd used last night and sipped the much-appreciated coffee. She would drink only half a cup and she intended to make it last as long as possible. "How long have you known Mrs. Matthews?"

Ida sat across from her with a cup of coffee filled with cream and sugar. "Maude and I grew up together. And I suggest you call her that instead of Mrs. Matthews." She paused and grinned at Beth's expression. "Now, you wouldn't be wondering how we grew up together, obviously being from different social circles, would you?"

Heat filled Beth's cheeks. "Um, well..."

Ida laughed and waved a hand. "Don't mind me. I never can resist that one. My mother was Maude's parents' housekeeper. Mom and I lived in the servants' quarters on their estate not far from here, and since Maude and I are a year apart in age, we played together.

"Of course we went to different schools, her being a Wellington and all, but once we both got home each day, it didn't matter a whit. When it was time for her to go away to finishing school, we both pitched fits." Ida sighed. "It didn't do any good. She left, and I went and got myself pregnant. Sorry mess that was, but you don't want to hear about it, and besides, I got myself a fine son out of the bargain."

She was wrong. Beth wanted very much to hear about Ida and how she had handled being a single woman, pregnant and then raising a child. But how did she urge her to continue without sounding nosy?

"Do you have other children?" Beth asked conversationally.

"A daughter. Later I married Ed Barnes, a sergeant in the Marines. He adopted my boy and then we had Amelia. We ended up traveling around a lot, transferring from one military base to the other. But Maude and I always kept in touch and when my Ed died five years ago, I came here to work for her and David. David Sr. had died soon after young David got out of law school. A second heart attack did him in, God rest his soul."

Beth had wondered about David's father, but of course would never have asked. David seemed awfully young to head such a large and prominent firm.

"How long were you a single parent?" She hoped that didn't sound too nosy.

"About five years. I'd met Ed right away but there was no way I wanted anything to do with a man." Ida chuckled. "I gave him a run for his money, I did."

Beth understood completely. If she never trusted a man, or even never dated again it would be too soon. She realized she was unconsciously rubbing her tummy and immediately stilled her hand. But what did it matter if they knew about the baby? David had probably explained to his mother by now, and if Maude knew, Beth bet Ida did, too.

And if not, what did Beth have to lose? After this morning, she'd never see these women again. Or David. The thought was oddly unsettling.

She recalled his reaction to her chaste kiss last night and how surprised she'd been at his obvious discomfort. It was both funny and sweet, and she'd fallen asleep with the warm fuzzy feeling that he'd actually been touched in some way.

But today was a new day, one of making hard decisions and moving forward. The thought scared her to death.

"Now I have a question for you." Ida stared at her over the rim of her cup. "Do you ever take that coat off?"

"Only if I have to." Beth sighed. "I'm traveling rather light these days."

Ida frowned in thoughtful silence for a moment, and then asked, "How long will you be staying?"

She glanced at her watch. "For about another hour."

"Nonsense." Maude swept into the kitchen, looking trim and vibrant in a red silk pantsuit, her hair upswept into a chic French twist. "Good morning, ladies."

"Well, it's about time Her Highness woke up." Ida winked at Beth. "I've made fresh coffee twice."

"I'll have you know I've been up for nearly two hours." She smiled at Beth's "good morning" as she poured herself a cup of java. "We have so much to do today. I have lists to write, calls to make."

Ida frowned. "I hope you're not talking about that foolish party again. David is not going to like it." Ida shook her head, her frown deepening. "Not one bit."

"No, I'm not talking about the party." She looked at Beth again. "I'm talking about shopping."

Beth took a hasty gulp. "I'll be out of your way in ten minutes."

"Nonsense." Mrs. Matthews waved her hand with an air of authority. She was clearly a woman used to getting her way. "You're going with me."

DAVID CLEARED off his desk, and then made a notation in his day planner for tomorrow's meeting with the mayor. Outside his office he heard the secretaries chattering as they locked their desks and turned off their computers, preparing to leave for the day.

Was it really only five? He glanced at the gold-framed desk clock, a birthday gift from Monique last year. She was a nice woman, sophisticated, attractive, a contract lawyer, whose company he'd always enjoyed. Too bad she got tired of trying to compete with his job. Not that he thought that was a problem, but she had, and that was enough to cool the relationship.

He glanced at the clock again. Five-o-three.

And then he stared at the phone. Where the hell were his mother and Beth? And why was Ida being so cryptic?

He'd called once right before lunch, and then an hour ago. All Ida would say is that the other two were out. He was tempted to call his mother's cell phone, but she never answered the damn thing. He doubted she even knew how to turn it on.

Besides, he never called in the middle of the day and he wasn't up to getting the third degree, even though it was perfectly logical that he'd want to know if Beth had left and if his mother had been successful in slipping her some money.

"'Night, Mr. Matthews.''

He looked up as Heather, the secretary his assistant hired last week, poked her head in the door. She was young, late-twenties, blond and with a build that wouldn't quit. Most of the guys in the office were salivating over her.

"Good night, Heather. Drive carefully.''

She gave him a radiant smile. A dangerous one. He quickly turned his attention back to the day planner. She wasn't the first secretary in the office with eyes for the boss. He had no illusions that he was God's gift. The money and power attracted them. He'd already traveled that road once, with only scars to show for it.

Long after Heather had left, he stared restlessly at the senseless words on the page. Dammit, he wasn't going to get any work done. He ought to just go home. So what if it was earlier than usual? It was his house. He had a right…

He packed up his briefcase, and then got into his private elevator without saying anything to the staff lingering in the office. Not accustomed to rush hour, he cursed the traffic bottling up the Golden Gate Bridge, but managed to dictate two memos by the time he turned into his driveway.

Marvin was washing the limo on the side of the house as David pulled into the garage. He was tempted to ask his mother's driver where she'd been all day, but then figured he'd find out soon enough.

And then it struck him. What he really wanted to know was whether Beth was still here. Not that it made any difference to him. Except that he'd warned his mother not to get attached. Beth wasn't a stray puppy she could keep around to pamper and dote upon.

But it wasn't even that so much. If Ida hadn't sounded as though she were guarding a national secret, he wouldn't be so curious...suspicious...that was a better description. He would never have left the office early. At least he'd had the sense to pack his briefcase with enough work to last the rest of the evening.

As soon as he opened the door to the kitchen he smelled the aroma of roasting meat. Garlic was in the air, too. Not something Ida usually used very much. No one was in the kitchen, and it had been so long since he'd gotten home this early, he didn't know if that was the norm or not.

He peeked into the living room, and then the family room. Not a soul was around. Laughter came from down the hall and he stopped to listen.

Beth was still here.

Her soft yet uninhibited laugh was unmistakable, and an unexpected sense of peace warmed him. Perhaps because he didn't have to wonder where she'd found shelter for the night. After all, no one was using the guest room....

His mother walked out of Beth's room, still laughing over something but immediately sobered upon seeing him. "David, you're home."

"So I am. Excuse me. I was about to change." He tried to sidestep her.

"David? Is anything wrong?"

"No. Why?"

"You haven't come home this early since…" She shrugged, her speculative gaze drawing toward Beth's room.

Great. Just great. "I have a lot of work to catch up on and the office was too distracting."

She smiled, nodded, her expression annoyingly patronizing. "We'll be having dinner in about half an hour. I'm delighted you can join us."

"I'm afraid that isn't possible—"

The words died when Beth walked out of the room. Her hair was down, the coat was gone and the way the lavender dress hugged her slim curves nearly knocked him off his feet.

She gave him a shy smile. "Hi."

"You're still here."

Her expression fell.

"David!" His mother's appalled voice jolted him.

Beth looked helplessly at her.

"I only meant—" He cleared his throat. "I was simply surprised."

"I had every intention of leaving this morning," Beth began, "but—"

"I talked her out of it."

David looked at his mother, her eyes narrowed in warning. He gave her a look of his own, one that meant they'd talk later. "I'll be in my study."

"Fine." His mother smiled. "I'll let you know when dinner is ready."

About to tell her he wouldn't be joining them, he glanced at Beth again. She did look rather stunning, her hair so shiny it looked like spun gold. The exhaustion and strain were gone from her face and she was much prettier than he'd first thought.

He could make time for dinner. Why not? By tomorrow she'd be gone. It wouldn't hurt him to be sociable for an hour.

"All right," he said and started to loosen his tie. "I'll go change and then check with you before I start in on my reading."

"Splendid." His mother clasped her hands together and looked adoringly at their guest. "We're in for a treat. Beth cooked tonight."

He frowned. "Is anything wrong with Ida?"

"No. Beth insisted as a sort of interview." His mother smiled. "I talked her into staying and filling in while Ida's gone."

Chapter Four

Beth couldn't imagine what everyone thought of dinner. The pork chops tasted like cardboard. Not even the rich brown mushroom sauce salvaged them. And the potatoes...oh, God they stuck in her throat like wallpaper glue.

"This meal is fabulous." Maude sat at the head of the table. She put down her fork and looked at Ida. "I thought you said pork chops were too dry, that's why you don't make them."

"They wouldn't be dry if you let me fix them proper like." Ida sniffed. "You're always too worried about fat and calories."

"This sauce doesn't taste fatty at all."

Ida cocked her head to the side. "No, it doesn't. What have you got in here, Beth?"

"Chicken stock thickened with pureed roasted vegetables instead of butter and flour. Lots of garlic, too."

They were being nice, probably didn't want to hurt her feelings. Why hadn't she left this morning? By now she could have been halfway to... Good question. She still hadn't figured that out yet. But she'd better do it quick. After this disastrous dinner, she'd be lucky to keep the temporary job.

Of course the possibility existed that dinner wasn't so horrible. That it only tasted that way to Beth because her mouth was drier than the Mojave Desert. Being nervous always did that to her.

She slid David a furtive glance. He sat silently at the other end of the table while the other two women chatted about sugar and carbohydrates. At least he had an appetite. In fact, he'd already polished off half the food on his plate. His expression hadn't changed though. He still had the same sullen look he'd had from the time his mother announced Beth would be staying.

"Beth?" Maude stared at her with concern.

"I'm sorry. Did you say something?"

Ida snorted, and Maude gave her a censuring look.

"I'd really like you to give Ida this recipe. David, isn't it wonderful?"

He nodded, and then took a sip of the wine he'd brought up from the cellar. When he hadn't poured any for Beth, Maude said nothing, but Ida asked if he'd forgotten his manners. Beth knew right then that he'd told his mother about the pregnancy. But no one had told Ida. That they had protected her privacy in that small way gave her a warm fuzzy feeling.

Maude sighed. "Really, David, you could show a little more enthusiasm for all the work Beth put into dinner."

Beth groaned inwardly.

"Speaking of work..." He set down his fork, pulled the napkin off his lap, folded it in two and set it beside his plate. "Thank you, Beth, for an outstanding meal."

He picked up his half-full wineglass as he stood. Beth's gaze drew to the snugness of his jeans and she quickly looked away.

"You can't leave yet," Maude said. "We haven't had dessert."

"I'll pass."

"You can't. Beth made a peach parfait."

"That's all right," Beth said quickly. "It'll keep."

David eyed her, his expression unreadable, and then his gaze swept the table. "Excuse me, ladies."

Maude started to say something, but refrained when Beth threw her a pleading look. No one said another word until David left, and then Ida spoke.

"That boy is going to work himself to death. He'll end up having a heart attack just like his daddy." She sent Maude an apologetic glance. "God rest his soul."

"Yes," Maude said absently, clearly distracted as she stared off after David. "But he did come home early. That's something."

"That it is." Ida glanced at Beth and then tried to hide a smile behind her napkin.

Beth saw it though and wondered what the heck that meant. "He probably wanted to make sure I'd left. I promised him I'd be gone today."

Maude's brows rose sharply. "David wouldn't expect you to leave with no place to go." Her gaze flickered. "He told me a little about your situation. I hope you don't mind."

Beth shook her head, and noticed that Ida's interest had suddenly piqued. Maude would have a time evading her questions. Beth didn't care. She set her barely touched food aside and stood.

Maude's concerned gaze met hers. "You haven't finished your dinner."

"I'll be back to clear the table after you've had dessert. It's in the fridge."

"But where are you going?"

Beth took a deep breath. She hated nothing worse than confrontation. "To talk to your son."

THE KNOCK at his study door was too soft to be either his mother or Ida. That left Beth. For a moment he thought about not answering. But that would be childish. Anyway, she'd corner him sooner or later.

He hadn't even opened his briefcase yet and he quickly placed a stack of papers on the desk in front of him. "Come in."

The door opened but he didn't look up right away. He made a production out of dragging his gaze away from the top sheet as if it were the answer to the national debt instead of a proposal for the company Christmas party.

"I know I'm bothering you but this can't wait."

The determination in Beth's voice surprised him and he leaned back and gave her his full attention. "No bother. Have a seat."

She tucked a strand of hair behind her ear with a nervous hand, and then lowered herself to the nearer of the two brown leather club chairs. She huddled to one side, leaving half the seat vacant.

"I'm sure you were disappointed I wasn't gone by the time you got home, but I'd like to explain." She shifted, crossing her legs. He tried not to look, but her hem rode up a few inches above her knees, capturing his interest.

"You see, your mother…" She hesitated, wrinkling her nose, no doubt searching for tact. "Well—"

"My mother could make Attila the Hun look like a cub scout when she has her mind set on something. You don't have to explain."

"But I do. I told you I'd be gone but she offered me the job of filling in for Ida and it seemed a great solution for both of us."

"Of course. It makes perfect sense."

"Then why do you look as though you want to bite my head off?"

David leaned back in his chair, admittedly feeling a little uneasy. Not angry. "I wasn't aware I appeared that way."

"It's the clothes, isn't it?"

"The clothes?"

She lifted her chin, tucked back her hair. "I'm paying her back every cent."

"I'm not following you."

"Your mother insisted we go shopping today. She bought me things." Beth visibly swallowed. "Expensive clothes that may take me a while to repay, but once I get a real job I'll send something every month."

"What my mother does with her money is none of my concern. Even if she wanted to buy you a house, it still wouldn't be my business."

"But you *are* upset."

"Not true. I had no idea you two went shopping

today, although knowing Mother, I should have guessed.''

Beth cocked her head to the side. ''So why are you in an icky mood? Was it the pork chops?''

He laughed. He couldn't help it. ''Dinner truly was terrific. If I've been 'icky,' I assure you it has nothing to do with you.''

She studied him, disbelief written all over her face. ''May I have a piece of paper and a pen?''

''Of course.'' He sat up and handed her a sheet of his personal stationery. ''This all right?''

She nodded. ''I'm writing you an I.O.U.''

''A what?''

''An I.O.U. It's a promise to pay—''

''I know what it is.'' His patience slipped. ''Is that how you handled things back in Idaho?''

Hurt flickered in her eyes. ''Back on the farm a promise and a handshake were enough.''

Dammit. He hadn't meant to sound critical or as if he were belittling her. If anything, her earnestness and accountability impressed him. She could've accepted his mother's generosity without a qualm, knowing they had money. In his business, he'd grown used to freeloaders and people looking for an easy buck.

Not Beth. She wanted to sign an I.O.U. And he hadn't a single doubt she'd make good on it.

He exhaled, rubbed his eyes. ''Beth, you're not going to write an I.O.U. Whatever my mother bought you, consider a gift.''

''Back on the farm, we don't accept charity, either.''

"I thought people helped their neighbors in small towns."

She blinked. "You aren't a neighbor. You're a stranger, really, and I'm embarrassed enough that I've had to depend on you." Her hand went to her stomach. "If it weren't for the baby, I wouldn't even—" She shook her head. "It doesn't matter. If you think it's a bad idea that I stay, I'll leave first thing in the morning."

His gaze lingered on the hand she had pressed to her slightly rounded belly. If she weren't so slim, no one would be able to guess her condition. She could get a job somewhere. A potential employer wouldn't have to know about her pregnancy.

David thought about his accountant. Didn't he have a clerk out on temporary disability? Maybe the timing would work out. And then what? Once Beth delivered the baby, what would she do about child care and medical insurance and...

Dammit! This was not his problem.

"David?"

He looked up and met her troubled eyes. Worry lines had formed between her brows.

"You're looking funny again."

"I was just thinking."

She took a deep breath, her breasts rising and falling and gaining his full attention. They weren't too large, but round and high. "If you have to think about it that long, then there really isn't anything to think about," she said and abruptly stood.

"What?" He stared absently for a moment. "No, it's not that. Please sit."

She shifted, her stance and expression hesitant before slowly lowering herself back to the chair.

He didn't understand his resistance. Filling in during Ida's absence was truly the perfect solution for both parties. His mother needed the help. Her kindness, wisdom and support meant the world to him, but when it came to domestic duties, she was hopeless.

Clueless, in fact. She'd gone from rich parents to a wealthy husband and never worked a day in her life. Her efforts on behalf of her pet charities, however, were tireless and unrelenting. Which worried him. Beth wasn't a project.

He understood his mother's desire to want to rescue and protect her. Her youth, her situation. He noticed the fullness of her breasts again, and the way the vee of her dress exposed the top of her cleavage.

Okay, so she wasn't that young. A totally inappropriate tug in his groin filled him with disgust and he forced his gaze away. Obviously he'd been celibate too long. Still, his reaction was inexcusable.

"David, if you'd rather I come back later—"

He straightened. "Why?"

She shook her head, while regarding him with curiosity. "You seem very distracted."

If she only knew… He cleared his throat. "I was wondering about your medical insurance."

Her expression fell, and she sighed.

"Or lack thereof…"

She nodded, her face miserable. "Lack thereof would be appropriate."

"That's a problem."

"Well, no kidding, Sherlock. When did you figure that out?"

Taken by surprise, he laughed.

Beth groaned and covered her face. "That was rude," she muttered. "I'm sorry."

"No need to apologize. You're right. That was an inane remark."

"Am I fired?"

He frowned, and then saw the twinkle in her eye and realized she was teasing. "On the contrary, I'm thinking I should add you on as an employee of the firm so that you'd be eligible for medical insurance."

Her eyes clouded with doubt.

"Of course you'd remain here to help my mother. Making you an employee would only be a technicality."

"But what about Tommy? He'd find out, wouldn't he?"

The surge of anger that assaulted David shocked him. He wasn't a violent man, but he'd love nothing more than to have his hands around Snyder's scrawny neck. "Tom isn't going to hurt you."

"I know," she said quickly, her eyes wary. "I only meant that his co-workers might find out about me. I don't want to cause trouble for him."

David's anger swelled. "Why the hell do you care if he's put out? Have you forgotten what he's done to you?"

Her hand went to her stomach again. "Hardly."

He pushed a hand through his hair. "I'm sorry. I was out of line."

"No, you weren't. You're trying to help." She

shrugged, a serene smile curving her lips. "But my dragging Tommy down isn't going to change anything between us. No matter what, he'll still be my baby's father. I hope someday they can have a relationship."

David felt like an idiot. She was right. He wasn't thinking logically. Which was totally atypical of him. Was his emotional reaction his subconscious way of making up for the past? If Kathy had had their child, it would be about nineteen now.

Only six years younger than Beth.

The reality slapped him in the face.

He inhaled deeply. "No one but the office manager needs to know, and only because she processes all the employees' paperwork."

Beth's smile reached her eyes, making them sparkle. "I guess that means I get to stay on."

"Whatever you worked out with my mother is fine with me. However, I think you should press Tom for financial support, both for prenatal care and later for the child."

"No way." She gave an emphatic shake of her head. "I won't do it."

"Right now you're angry, but think about it. No acrimony need be involved." He paused. "There doesn't have to be any bitterness or animosity."

"I know what acrimony means," she said crisply. "He won't even give me the money he owes me. That's all I wanted in the first place."

"Legally you could compel him to help—" He gritted his teeth when she started shaking her head again. Dammit. He wanted her to stick up for herself. Not be a doormat. "This isn't about dragging him through the mud or revenge. It's your legal right. After all, he abandoned you.''

Her mouth lifted in a wry smile. "No, he didn't."

That she could still defend the guy made David see red. "If you recall, I heard most of your conversation last night."

"I left him."

David frowned. "But you said—" He tried to think back. Hadn't she asked Tom to…?

"Last night I asked him to repay some money he took from me. I never asked him to let me go back." She sat with a serene expression, the picture of composure. "When I told him I was pregnant, he got nasty and told me to get rid of the baby. I refused and he got even nastier.

"Up until that point, I'd seen some of the changes in him but I kept telling myself he was under a lot of pressure with his new job and it would all blow over. But when he became abusive—"

David clenched his fists. "He hit you?"

"No, but he was verbally abusive. I didn't deserve the things he said." She lifted her chin. "I certainly wasn't going to take any of that garbage. So I packed a few things and left." Her shoulders slumped. "Unfortunately I then found out that he'd maxed out my credit cards and drained my bank account. I had a little cash but not enough to get far."

"That's called theft." His temper ignited, he barely managed to speak in a civil tone.

She shrugged. "Not exactly. He still had student loans to pay, but he needed clothes and such for his job, and so I gave him access to my accounts. Of course I never dreamed he'd milk me dry.'' Sighing, she bowed her head. "I was stupid and naïve at first. But I wasn't about to hang around for any more of his ugliness.''

She lifted her chin again and met his gaze. Determination and strength shone in her eyes, and David's respect and admiration for her rose three notches. Some doormat. Hell, had he been wrong about her.

"You're a remarkable woman, Beth Anderson."

She blushed. "Right. That's why I landed in this mess.''

"It could have been worse. You could've stayed."

"No chance."

He smiled. That's what made her remarkable. "Okay, so for now we leave the—Tom alone.''

She grinned at his near slip of the tongue.

"But tomorrow I'm getting you signed up for company benefits. It'll be totally kosher. Mother and I own the firm.''

Beth stared at him for a moment, her eyes bright, and he prayed she didn't start crying. "Thank you."

Silence lengthened, allowing time for panic to set in. He had no idea where it came from, or why tension painfully tightened his chest. "Look, there is another option. I could give you the money to leave town and get set up somewhere, maybe closer to Rock Falls.''

A stricken look crossed her face.

"It would be loan," he added, knowing that would be the only way she'd accept the money.

She clasped her hands together, hunched her shoulders and looked around as if searching for something to say.

The simple, helpless movement reduced him to soggy oatmeal. He'd never felt at such a loss in his life.

"I appreciate your generous offer." She stood abruptly. "But I'll have to pass."

"It was only a suggestion."

A sad smile touched the corners of her mouth and she backed up. "I'll stick to my original plan of leaving tomorrow. I'm sure your mother can find some other help."

"Beth." He got up and rounded the desk in time to block her way out. "You misunderstand me."

She shook her head, and lowered her gaze. "I should have discussed your mother's offer with you before I accepted. I'm a stranger. If you don't want me in your house, I understand. Really."

He touched her chin with his finger and brought her head up. She kept her lids lowered. "That is not the case. *Really.*"

She looked at him, surprise chasing away the wariness.

He smiled. "I didn't want you to feel this was your only option if you'd rather be back in Iowa."

A small grin tugged at her mouth. "Idaho."

"Forgive me."

She let the smile blossom. It reached her eyes, making the blue so vivid it made him tense. He lowered his hand.

She blinked, and the uncertainty returned.

"There's something else I meant to tell you," he said, and this time she tensed. "I'm glad you went shopping today. That dress is—you look beautiful."

With a shy, endearing smile, she went up on tiptoes and flattened a palm on his chest. His hand automatically went to her waist, his heart rate accelerating.

"Thank you." She lightly kissed his cheek, dropped her hand and then moved back.

God almighty, what was wrong with him? He'd wanted to kiss her. Not like the brotherly peck she'd given him. He wanted to feel her rounded breasts under his palms. He wanted...

Shaken, he stepped back, as well. "Now, if you'll excuse me, I have a lot of work to do."

Chapter Five

Beth went straight to her room. She knew Maude and Ida were gabbing in the kitchen and she needed to be alone for a few minutes. At least long enough to recover some strength back in her knees, and to get her hands to quit shaking.

Darn her hormones. She was losing it. For a moment she'd thought David was going to kiss her. If that wasn't bad enough she'd actually *wanted* him to kiss her. On the mouth. Like a lover would. In fact, she'd almost kissed him. Oh, boy was she going off the deep end. If he had any inkling of her errant feelings, he'd no doubt send her packing.

Thank goodness she hadn't made a fool of herself. It was obvious what had happened, or what could happen if she weren't careful. She was reacting to what David symbolized. He made her feel safe, protected. He wanted to fight for her rights. After her experience with Tommy, it felt good to know someone cared.

Of course, it wasn't really personal with David. She was vulnerable, and he was a good man who would always defend the weak, no matter who it was. She knew darn well he perceived her as young and naïve.

That was partly true, except she wasn't the martyr he thought her to be.

If he could peek into her thoughts, the ones that came from the dark side, he'd be shocked. She didn't want to protect Tommy; she wanted to strangle him. How many nights had she lain awake plotting some kind of torturous revenge? But ultimately she'd decided that his having to live in his own miserable skin was revenge enough. Besides, what she'd told David was true. Some day maybe Tommy would grow up and be able to have a relationship with his child.

She sat on the edge of her bed and massaged her lower back. She'd been on her feet a long time today. Maude had the energy and stamina of a twenty-year-old. At least when it came to shopping.

Beth eyed the array of packages on the dresser and pink floral chair. There were at least a dozen tote bags and that didn't take into account the bags in the closet. How she was going to repay all this she had no idea. She would, though, no matter how long it took.

After the third boutique she'd been afraid to look at price tags anymore. Discount shops and the occasional department store were Beth's usual haunts. Mostly because that's all she could afford. She doubted Maude had ever been in one. The clerks in every boutique knew her by name and were quick to do her bidding. It was a little nerve-wracking.

Probing her sore muscles with her fingers, Beth found a particularly nasty knot near her lower backbone. She tried to work it out but it was useless. Instead she forced herself to stand, and then stretched.

As much as she'd love to hide out for the evening, she'd promised to clear the table.

Besides, she had to have a talk with Maude. Maybe staying wasn't the right thing to do.

MAUDE KNOCKED on her son's door. She had a few words for him, and she didn't care how much work he had to do. What she had to say wouldn't keep until morning. She didn't wait for him to answer before she barged into his study.

He was leaning back in his chair, his hands clasped behind his neck as he stared at the ceiling.

"David?"

He looked absently at her.

How odd. She figured he'd be busy at work as usual. She hoped he wasn't ill. Of course since yesterday, he'd been full of surprises. "What are you doing?"

"Thinking."

"About what? Other ways to upset me and our guest?"

His left eyebrow went up, just like his father's used to when he was in one of his haughty moods. "I'm sure you'll explain what you're talking about."

"What did you do to Beth?"

Wariness flickered in his eyes and he straightened. "What do you mean?"

She sat in one of the leather chairs. Something was going on here. Something more than Beth had admitted. "I want to know what you said to her that's changed her mind about staying?"

He frowned. "She's leaving?"

Fascinated with his reaction, she chose her words carefully. "This afternoon she thought it was a good idea to stay and fill in for Ida. After her talk with you, she changed her mind."

He muttered a curse.

"David!"

"Sorry." He passed a hand over his face, blew into his palm.

"And that's not all." She gave him a stern, all-knowing look—the one that prompted many a high school confession.

After a calculated silence, he sighed with disgust. "She told you about the kiss."

Maude nearly slid off the chair. "You kissed Beth?"

"No."

"She kissed you?"

Dread and regret crawled across his face. Just like when he was in the eighth grade and impulsively owned up to looking at a friend's girlie magazine. "It wasn't what you're thinking."

She tried not to smile. "I'm listening."

"There's nothing to explain. Nothing happened."

"You brought up the kiss. Not me."

"There was no kiss. I just thought maybe she—" He broke off and then muttered, "She kissed me on the cheek."

She eyed him with suspicion but he remained stubbornly silent, making her long for the old days when David actually confided in her. Finally, she could stand it no more. "David Elliot Matthews, there's something you aren't telling me."

He rubbed his eyes. "Why did she say she's leaving?"

"She didn't, only that it might be a good idea."

"I offered her money so she could go back to Idaho."

"Now, why on earth would you do that?" Maude glared at her son. "We had it all settled that she'd stay here while Ida was gone. And I'll tell you something else. Ida isn't getting any younger. It just may be that she'll need the help permanently."

"You mean Beth?"

"Who do you think I mean?"

With a grunt, he turned away, but she caught his unsettled expression. Beth had gotten to him.

For the past few years, David had behaved more like a robot then a young man. He went to work early, came home late and the only discussions that interested him were about the firm's latest high-profile case or the increase in revenue. She understood what pushed him to make the firm the biggest and best in the city. His father. David idolized the man to a fault.

His father had been far more fallible than David realized.

"Look, Mother, I know you want to help. I do, too. But Beth is a grown woman. She can make her own decisions. She doesn't need you or me orchestrating her life."

Maude sniffed as his presumption. "Are you finished with your unsolicited dissertation?"

"I'll go talk to her."

"Oh, good. You've had so much success in that department already."

"Sarcasm is not your style, Mother." He gave her a long probing look. "Don't take too great an interest in Beth. It wouldn't be wise to get emotionally involved."

Maude met and held his gaze. "What about you, David? How much of an interest are you taking?"

"What is that supposed to mean?" He stared back, his eyes challenging, but he didn't fool her. She knew him too well. The tiny twitch at the corner of his mouth gave him away. "I invited her to spend one night. That's all. You, on the other hand, have decided to make her some kind of rescue project."

"That's not fair. And God help you if she ever hears you say anything like that again. That poor girl's pride has been bruised enough."

Curiosity flickered in his eyes. "What has she told you?"

Ignoring him, Maude gestured to the carafe of water he kept on his credenza. "Be a love and pour me some of that."

He hesitated, and then finally swiveled around to the credenza. Patience had never been one of his virtues. Maybe he'd break down and really talk to her like he had when he was a kid before adolescence made her the enemy.

More importantly, she wanted to fan the spark that had ignited in him. It'd been too long since she'd seen any passion or humanity in his eyes. He'd gone from hellion to choirboy to workaholic with each dramatic turning point in his life. Perhaps fate had thrown in a certain pretty blue-eyed blonde to balance the picture. She hoped so.

She'd studied Beth all day. Maude didn't impress easily, but this young woman had her smitten. Not only was Beth well mannered and genuinely kind, she embodied the old work ethic, with her earnest desire to pull her own weight, instead of lobbying for a pass to climb the social ladder.

Maude sighed to herself. Very few young ladies fell into that category anymore. Not like when she'd been that age.

He handed her the glass of water. "Well?"

She raised questioning brows.

"Mother." He drawled her name into a warning.

"Oh, yes, we were talking about my chat with Beth." Maude took a leisurely sip. "I really don't feel comfortable discussing anything she told me. It was in confidence." She gave him her best innocent look. "But I'm quite sure that if you asked her…"

"Okay, you've had your fun." Clearly annoyed, David stood, and Maude forced back a smile.

"Fun? Pardon me, but do you think it's fun for an old woman to have to wait around for grandchildren?"

His jaw slackened. "How much wine have you had tonight?"

She bristled. He should have challenged the "old woman" reference.

"You get that out of your head immediately. Beth is too young for me." His gaze hardened, so much like his father's. "She's naïve and unsophisticated and still very innocent." He paced toward the window, shoved aside the drapes with a restless hand and stared out at the city lights for a moment. "I offered to take her in out of charity and nothing more. Do you understand?''

''Perfectly.'' Maude chuckled. ''Who said I was referring to Beth? It does make me wonder why you're protesting so vehemently.''

DAVID STOOD at the kitchen door watching Beth load the dishwasher. He'd overheard her giving Ida firm instructions to go put her feet up and watch some television. Ida finally conceded, admitting her favorite program was about to start.

His mother was right. Ida probably needed the help. Other than the more strenuous jobs like carpet cleaning and window washing, she insisted on handling all the domestic chores herself. It wasn't all that much for only the three of them, but still...

Beth loaded the dinner plates, and then stopped suddenly and straightened. Pressing a hand to her lower back, she massaged the area, making soft noises of relief.

''I bet Mother had you on your feet all day.''

She lowered her hand and turned, her eyes wide. ''You startled me.''

''Sorry.'' He went to the fridge and took out the rest of the wine from dinner. ''Can I get you anything?''

''No, thanks,'' she mumbled and turned back to the dishwasher.

''Orange juice?''

''No, really. I'm fine.''

He pulled out a kitchen chair. ''Would you sit with me?''

She stared at the chair as if it might have electric currents running through it. "I have to finish the dishes."

"Later," he said, and when she shook her head, he added, "I'll help."

That made her smile. "When was the last time you loaded a dishwasher?"

"How is that relevant?"

Her eyes sparkled with amusement. "Have you *ever* done it?"

"Is there a point to all this?"

"You haven't?" Her eyebrows shot up, and then she shrugged. "I guess there's no reason you should."

"Now that you've made me feel totally useless, the least you can do is sit."

She laughed. "Yeah, because you're such a lazy bum who's never put in a full day's work in his life."

David smiled. She'd surprised him. No apology, no backpedaling, no blushing. "Are you going to sit or do I have to pick you up and seat you myself?"

That got a reaction. She stiffened, gave him a you-wouldn't-dare look and then promptly sat.

He took the chair across from her and poured himself half a glass of wine. "Are you sure I can't get you anything?"

She gave him a funny smile, as though she found him amusing, or as if she knew something he didn't. "No, thank you."

"Fine, then let's get down to business."

She frowned. "Business?"

"What was this you told my mother about not staying? I thought we had your employment settled."

"Well, we did, sort of." She folded her hands together and rested them on the table, her gaze steady on his face.

"I'm listening."

"I reconsidered."

"Just like that?"

She blinked, her throat working as she swallowed. "I thought it best."

"For whom?"

"Probably both of us."

David cursed to himself. She'd known he wanted to kiss her, or that the thought had crossed his mind. He should bring it out in the open, set the record straight. "I work long hours. I'm rarely home. It makes no difference to me."

"That's what your mother said."

They'd discussed him? Great. "Then it must be true, right?"

She laughed, making her entire expression change from tense to youthful and happy. "Mothers never lie."

"Right." He grunted, thinking back on his ill-spent youth and his mother's all-out attempts to reel him in. "You remember that later."

Her good humor faded, and her hand went to her stomach. "Sometimes it's hard to believe it's real."

The familiar words were like an unexpected blow. They could have been uttered yesterday instead of twenty years ago. Kathy had sat beside him in his first car, a red BMW convertible he'd gotten for his seventeenth birthday, when she'd told him she was pregnant.

He'd thought it was a joke. She'd assured him it wasn't, and they'd spent the better part of the night trying to figure out what to do. At the time they were both in college, and after that, he still had three years of law school ahead of him. Kathy had wanted to get married. He'd wanted to run as fast as he could.

"I'm not complaining," Beth said, studying him with uncertainty and clearly misreading his preoccupation. "I've always wanted kids. Tons of them. It's just that I haven't finished school yet, and well..." She lifted her shoulders in a helpless gesture. "This wasn't planned."

The way she averted her gaze told him there was more to it. Probably more than he wanted to know. He should leave it alone. "And you don't love Tom."

She drew her head back, her eyes wide, but she couldn't be half as surprised as he was that he'd made such a personal remark. "No, I don't." Color rose in her cheeks. "Which of course makes you wonder why I slept with him."

"No." He held up a hand. Dammit, he knew better. It wasn't even like him to be curious. He was supposed to be clearing the air between them, not stirring up more tension. "None of my business."

She gave him a dry look.

"You're right. I shouldn't have commented in the first place."

"Tommy is the only guy I've ever slept with." She stared down at her hands. "I've known him for fifteen years." She gave a short bitter laugh. "Or at least I thought I knew him."

"This really isn't necessary." David clenched his

jaw. She'd been a virgin and the bastard had taken full advantage of her. But the guy was still an employee and David was a fool to be listening, or getting involved.

"It is for me. I don't want you to think I'm promiscuous."

"First, the thought never occurred to me. Second, you don't owe me a single explanation."

Her lips lifted in a shy smile. "It's kind of nice to have someone to talk to. You remind me of my brother, minus the temper."

"Ah." David sipped his wine, mentally shaking his head at himself. It could be worse, he supposed. She could have likened him to her father.

"Junior didn't always have a short fuse. Well, I guess he did, but he could control it better. But then the farm started having financial trouble, and feed prices went up and the kids needed braces and..." She made a wry face. "Sorry, you don't want to hear all this."

He waved a hand. "Feel free." After all, he was practically one of the family.

Her remark about her brother chafed. It was David's upcoming birthday that was the real problem. If only his mother wouldn't make such a big deal out of it. The day could come and go and it would be business as usual.

Fortunately she hadn't mentioned the party in a while. He'd warned her that would be the last straw. Maybe he'd finally gotten through to her. Or maybe Ida had talked some sense into her.

"You're still upset, aren't you?" Beth asked quietly, and when he looked at her, he saw the color rushing to her cheeks. "I'm sorry," she blurted, looking genuinely distraught, her hands fidgety, her eyes anxious. "I'm really, really sorry. I don't know what came over me."

David stared blankly at her. He didn't have the faintest idea what she was talking about.

She lowered her gaze and picked furiously at a loose thread on the blue woven place mat. "I hate to keep blaming hormones but there's no other explanation. I'm sure I scared the heck out of you. I can only promise it won't happen again."

Was he being dense? What had he missed? "What happened?"

She raised her reluctant gaze by degrees, and then cleared her throat. "In your den?"

He frowned. "In my den."

"You don't have to make this so difficult." Her tone went from sheepish to crisp. "I did apologize." She sighed. "Sorry for snapping."

"You seem to think I'm being coy. I assure you I have no idea what you're talking about."

A hopeful glint lit Beth's eyes. "Really?"

He nodded slowly, his curiosity growing.

Relief eased the tension around her mouth. "Leave it to me to worry about nothing. Unfortunately, that I can't blame on hormones."

David waited a few moments, hoping she'd continue. She didn't. "What did you think happened?"

Her eyes widened. "Uh-uh, no way. If you don't know, then I'm not telling." Her gaze lowered to his mouth, lingered and then she quickly looked away and got up from the table as if she'd been caught rifling through the cookie jar.

An absurd thought struck him. Had *she* wanted to kiss *him?*

No, couldn't be.

He watched her attack the dishwasher, her cheeks a bright pink. God help him, he was in trouble.

Chapter Six

One week to the day. David stared at his desk calendar. One week since his life had been normal, since he'd been able to give the firm his full concentration. His workdays were getting shorter, and God help him he'd even taken half of Saturday and all of Sunday off.

He was tired. He hadn't taken time off in three years and the fourteen-hour days were finally getting to him. It had nothing to do with age, or Beth, or anything else. He was human, and he was tired. Period.

Flipping to tomorrow's page, he groaned. How the hell had he booked two lunches? Why hadn't his secretary caught it? Obviously because he hadn't told her about it, just like he'd forgotten to tell her to expect the mayor's conference call yesterday.

He was losing it, and everyone in the office probably knew it. Dammit.

Rest…lots of rest. That's what he needed. Maybe he'd book a Mediterranean cruise. That would be a good thing to do for his birthday. He'd get away from any of his mother's shenanigans, and it would force him to slow down at the same time.

Nah, that would take too much time. A weekend in the Caribbean perhaps, where there was no fog or fall chill in the air.

He closed his eyes and pinched the bridge of his nose. He knew he wouldn't go. The idea didn't even sound all that good. He'd just keep doing what he'd been doing this week. Cut back a little on work. Get into bed at a decent hour with a good book. He'd feel like his old self in no time.

Wisely his mother had said nothing about his more frequent appearances around the house. Ida had left for her vacation three days ago so he didn't have to contend with her typically brash observations. And of course there was Beth, who largely acted as though he didn't exist.

Which was fine with him. The less contact they had the better. The problem was, even when she wasn't around, he was still very much aware of her presence. The rooms smelled like jasmine. It wasn't his imagination, or the fresh flowers she picked from the garden each day and placed in vases around the house. She had a distinct scent.

"Mr. Matthews?"

He looked up to find Heather staring quizzically at him. "Yes?"

"Is there anything I can do for you?" Her rich golden tan made her smile blindingly white.

"No, why?"

She flinched at his impatient tone. "Cassie went to lunch. She asked me to cover for her."

David sighed. He was being an ass. His assistant always made sure one of the secretaries was available to him when she wasn't. But he'd have to remember to ask her to eliminate Heather from the pool.

She was certainly sharp enough, very competent from what he could tell, but she was a little too brazen. She was pretty, but she knew it. And flaunted it. From the clothes she wore to the prolonged eye contact, to the casual arm touching, the woman obviously had a game plan.

He couldn't imagine Beth ever behaving that way, and she was every bit as pretty as Heather...prettier, actually. Her hair was that unusual honey color which he'd bet his Jaguar was natural. And her eyes...God, he'd never seen eyes so blue...

"I guess I'll just go back to my desk." Heather gave him a worried look as she backed out of the office door. "Buzz if you need anything."

He snapped out of his preoccupation. "One thing. Is Tom Snyder back from Chicago?"

"I think I saw him in his office this morning."

"Tell him I'd like to see him."

Her megawatt smile was back. "Right away."

"Thank you, Heather."

"Sure, boss." She lifted one slim shoulder in a blatantly flirtatious manner. Another quarter of an inch and her blouse would be cut too low, the silk too tight around her breasts. "Anything else I can do for you?"

"That's all." He went back to studying his calendar until he knew she'd left. And then realized he'd booked two more appointments at the same time on Friday.

He'd barely had time to kick himself when Tom Snyder knocked at his open door.

"You wanted to see me, sir?" Tom flashed him that smile that had all the secretaries reapplying their lipstick every hour.

He was a good-looking enough guy, David supposed, a charmer that had quickly earned him the reputation of being the office Casanova, according to Cassie. It had also netted him key accounts with two important female clients.

David didn't give a damn. The guy walked a fine line. That he hadn't found a reason to fire him yet was for Beth's sake.

"Come in, Tom." A civil tone was almost out of David's grasp, but he managed not to bite the guy's head off. "Have a seat."

"You probably want to know what's happening with the Clinton case." His charcoal-gray suit was Armani and his shoes looked like Gucci. Not something most young attorneys could afford. But of course, Snyder had helped himself to Beth's money.

David took a deep calming breath. This wasn't going to be easy. "How's the case going?"

Tom took a seat, leaned back and locked his hands behind his head. "Piece of cake. I doubt we even go to trial."

His smug arrogance chafed. It made it difficult for David to keep the condemnation out of his voice. "Glad to hear the case is going well, but that's not why I asked you in here."

Tom unclasped his hands and straightened. "Is anything wrong, sir?"

"I'll let you be the judge of that."

David hesitated, and apprehension creased Tom's

face. Good. The guy deserved to sweat. David adjusted his day planner, taking his time, making sure it lined up with his calendar before he said, "It's about Beth."

"Beth?" Shock, then wariness registered in Tom's eyes.

"Beth Anderson."

Tom paled, giving David enormous satisfaction. "What about her?"

"You do know her?"

Denial leapt into his face, and then indecision, finally anger. "Did she come here to see you?"

"No."

Tom clearly didn't know how to respond. He tugged at his tie, loosened his collar. "Beth has been emotional and unreasonable lately." He flashed an apologetic smile. "I hope she hasn't bothered you."

"I haven't found her to be unreasonable at all. Actually, she seems to have a pretty good head on her shoulders."

Tom's expression darkened. "When did you see her?"

"That's not important." David made a notation in his day planner. Nothing urgent. Just enough of an interruption to let Snyder stew. "What do you intend to do?"

He drew his head back slightly, looking confused and obviously wondering how much David knew.

David held his gaze. "Of course you realize you have a legal obligation."

Snyder's mouth tightened. "Do you know where she is? I want to talk to her."

"I don't believe that's an option."

"Is that what she said?" Snyder's arrogant surprise just about undid David's restraint.

He took a deep calming breath. "I believe the lady said something about never wanting to see you again."

"We had a quarrel." Tom shook his head, his mouth curving in a persuasive smile that probably worked on most people. "It was silly. I'm sure I can straighten everything out if you'll just tell me where she is."

"That isn't my call."

"I love her. I want her back." Snyder's attempt to look earnest fell short. If anything, he looked desperate.

Unable to take any more of the lying scumbag, David closed his day planner and put it in his briefcase. What had she seen in him? Beth wasn't like the other women in the office who were taken with the guy's dark good looks and quick wit.

Of course people changed. God knows David had made an about-face. Beth wouldn't have given him the time of day twenty years ago. He'd been brash, arrogant and self-centered. Kathy Miller had made the mistake of giving him more than that, and all it got her was heartache and a miscarriage.

Damn.

He couldn't think about that right now. This was about Beth, and protecting her rights. She didn't understand what she was in for once the baby was born. She'd need help, and Snyder damn well owed it to her.

He kept loading his briefcase, aware that Snyder

watched him with a gratifying mixture of apprehension and animosity.

"That's all for now," David said without looking up.

Snyder hesitated, but stood when David snapped his briefcase shut and rolled back from his desk. "Sir, is my job in jeopardy?"

"Of course not," David said in a deceptively amicable tone. And then he looked up to make sure Snyder saw the warning in his eyes. "It would be unethical and illegal to fire you over a personal matter. Anyway, you need to be gainfully employed. Child support can cost a fortune."

BETH CHECKED the caterer's list for the second time. Maude had ordered an awful lot of hors d'oeuvres for David's birthday party. Back home when they had get-togethers it was usually potluck and everyone brought things like fried chicken and potato salad.

Obviously she knew Maude and David lived in a different world, but that didn't help Beth understand how much escargot or pâté or jumbo shrimp was needed for a hundred people. Of course the caterers figured out that kind of stuff, but Maude had put Beth in charge of the caterers, and heavens, but she didn't want to screw up this party.

Maude was beside herself making sure every preparation was in place and that the affair would be a total surprise to David. How he would feel about it, Beth didn't know. But from a few comments Ida had made before she left, Beth guessed he wouldn't be too keen on being made the center of attention. In fact, he wasn't happy about turning forty.

Beth didn't understand why. He didn't act or look that old. Isn't that what counted? Although admittedly, not long ago she'd thought thirty was ancient. She leaned back in the huge black leather chair, put her feet up on the matching ottoman, and absently rubbed her rounded tummy. But so much had changed and she felt a whole lot more grown-up now.

"How are you coming along?" Maude swept into the library in a cloud of lilac. She always smelled so good.

"Fine. I think." Beth started to straighten but Maude waved her to sit back, and then took the other chair. "Are you sure you haven't ordered too much food?"

Maude laughed. "It's free. People will eat it. Trust me. How are you feeling?"

"Great." She moved her hand from her tummy. She was always rubbing there or her lower back, more from habit than anything else. Although when she stood too long, her back did give her some trouble. "I have to call the florist this afternoon."

"Something else occurred to me." Maude frowned as her gaze scanned the crowded floor-to-ceiling bookshelves. "I've got to call a contractor, or some such person. We're supposed to have this room painted. I imagine it should be done before the party. What do you think?"

"Is that possible?" Beth didn't know anything about hiring contractors. On the farm, they always did their own repairs.

Maude's smile was wry. "For the right price, anything's possible, but I'm wondering if you'd have time to work on it."

Beth shrugged helplessly. "I wouldn't know where to begin."

"Oh, honey, just when I was beginning to think you could do anything."

She frowned, not sure how to take Maude's remark.

The older woman leaned forward and squeezed her hand. "Have I told you what a great help you've been? I don't have the faintest idea how I would have managed without you."

Heat climbed Beth's face. "You're exaggerating, but thank you."

"Nonsense." Maude squeezed her hand once more and then released it, the sincerity in her eyes saying more than her words. "Besides, I've thoroughly enjoyed your company."

Darn it, darn it, darn it. Emotion welled in Beth's chest. How long would she be so touchy? For another six months? She swallowed hard, hoping Maude hadn't noticed the threat of tears.

Thankfully, she was busy looking around, likely mentally calculating what needed to be done.

"Yes, a fresh coat of paint will make everything look brighter. And maybe we should have the floors polished again. David spends so much time in here when he isn't working in his study. He loves this room."

So did Beth. That's why she spent most of her days here, checking lists, making phone calls between fixing the meals. She loved having such a large assortment of books at her fingertips. She'd even managed to read *Wuthering Heights* and *Sense and Sensibility* each for the third time.

She'd certainly had the occasion. What with David ignoring her every evening. Even Maude had noticed and made excuses for him. She hadn't come out and said anything specific, just that David was always very busy and that she was surprised he'd been making it home at a decent hour all week.

Of course Beth knew the real reason he was avoiding her. He probably thought she wanted to kiss him again. Just the thought brought heat to her face.

"Don't you agree?"

Beth snapped out of her preoccupation to find Maude frowning at her. "I'm sorry. I lost my train of thought," she mumbled.

The older woman's pink tinted lips curved into a kindly smile. "We were talking about getting a contractor tomorrow."

"Oh, yes, I'll take care of it." She had no idea where to begin but she'd figure it out.

"I believe David has a list of men who originally worked on the house. Perhaps one of them would be interested in the job."

"Won't he get suspicious?"

"Heavens, no. We'd talked about some cosmetic touch-ups around the house about a month ago."

Great. Beth had hoped to get out of having to deal with him.

"Of course don't let on how quickly we need to get this done or then he may get suspicious." Maude paused, and turned suddenly toward the door. "Did you hear something?"

"No, but it could be Mr. Ito. He's pruning the trees outside the patio where the caterer will be setting up tables and—"

The unmistakable slam of the door connecting the house and garage made both women jump. It had to be David.

Beth quickly gathered up the catering order and anything pertaining to the party. She hadn't even started dinner yet and he was home already?

"Whatever has gotten into that son of mine?" Maude stood, smoothed out her cream colored slacks. "Take your time. I'll go tend to him."

Beth took a deep breath and continued to collect her paperwork. It was time to start the lamb chops, anyway. Besides, hanging out in the kitchen was relatively safe. He rarely lingered there, and the less she saw of him the better.

Maude stopped at the door. "I'm afraid I'm going to have to add another chore to your list."

"Anything."

"If David keeps coming home early like this, he's going to need a distraction. You'll be perfect."

THE AROMA of garlic and lamb wafted into the den and had David reading the same paragraph twice. His stomach rumbled. Ida was a decent enough cook, but definitely lacking in imagination. Beth had no fear in the kitchen. She dumped spices into everything she cooked with excellent results. He actually looked forward to coming home to dinner every night, instead of having the corner deli send something to his office.

Since he wasn't getting anywhere with the brief that was beginning to blur before his eyes, he got up, stretched and then headed for the kitchen. He stopped outside the library door when he heard voices. One obviously belonged to Beth and the other was so heavily accented David couldn't recognize it.

The door was open so he casually walked past. Sitting across from Beth at the antique mahogany desk was a small Oriental man. His weathered brown face was creased in concentration as he stared at a piece of paper to which Beth pointed.

"Take your time," she was saying, each word slow and deliberate. "Sound out each letter slowly."

The man gave her a short nod and did as she asked.

Ah, David recognized him. He was their gardener. Kinji, David thought his name was, or something like that. If he remembered correctly, the man spoke little English, but he did an excellent job with the landscaping.

"That was very good, Mr. Ito." Beth beamed at him. "You're getting better and better every day."

The man's face split into a wide grin. He said something in Japanese and gave her a quick bow.

She repeated what he'd said and bowed in kind.

When she looked up again, she apparently noticed David and swung a startled look his way. The gardener followed her gaze, and upon seeing David, quickly rose.

"Good evening, Mr. Matthews," the man said, his

English broken. "Nice to see you." He glanced at Beth, clearly looking for approval.

She clapped her hands. "That was wonderful." She turned to David. "Wasn't that terrific?"

He stared back at her, knowing he should say something but too enthralled with the way her face lit up. Like fine blue sapphires, her eyes sparkled with excitement, and her face had flushed to a pretty rose color.

"Yes," David finally said to their expectant looks. "That was very good." He refrained from using Kinji's name in case his memory was faulty.

Beth gave him an odd look. Kinji seemed nervous. David sighed. What had he done wrong?

"I go now," Kinji mumbled, and headed for the door, his head down.

"Don't forget, we'll continue tomorrow afternoon," Beth called after him. And then she turned to David, her mouth a straight line of disapproval. "Your mother said it was all right for us to use the library."

He shrugged. "Okay."

"Then why did you look so—bothered?"

He snorted. "I hadn't realized I did."

"Poor Mr. Ito probably thinks he isn't welcome now." She picked up a stack of papers and shoved them into a folder. "Just when he was making so much progress."

"I'll speak to him if it will help."

She slid him a skeptical look.

"Believe it or not, I can be very diplomatic when I want to be."

"Really?" She hugged the folder to her chest and brushed past him.

He frowned at her retreating form. "What do you mean, really?"

She didn't stop but disappeared into the hall. He thought about letting the remark go, and then followed her to the kitchen.

"I'm sure you didn't mean to run off without answering my question," he said with a pleasant smile.

She'd been tying an apron around her waist. Her arms were bent behind her, making her breasts jut out against the thin fabric of her white T-shirt. Some lace showed through, as well as the outline of her nipples.

He wanted to see her naked.

The sudden and inappropriate thought shook him to the core and he sucked in a breath.

She finished tying her apron. "Oh, and what question was that?"

"Huh?"

Her gaze narrowed. "David?"

He took in another breath. Deeper this time. "Never mind."

"Are you all right?"

"Of course." He looked away, and went to the refrigerator. "What time's dinner?"

"In about fifteen minutes." She paused. "David?"

The tone of her voice filled him with dread. Soft...tentative...inquiring, it was like a prelude, no an ambush, to a cross-examination. Without getting a drink he closed the refrigerator door. "I'll be in the den."

"Wait."

Dammit. Reluctantly, he faced her.

"Did I do something wrong?" Concern etched two lines between her brows. "We didn't touch anything in the library. We just used the desk."

"I don't have a problem with you using the library. Hell, feel free to touch anything you want in there."

She flinched a little. "But you gave us such a stern look."

His laugh was without humor. "I was feeling far from stern. I was admiring you."

She blinked. "Me?"

"Your patience, your generosity of spirit…"

Her face instantly flooded with color and she grabbed a dishtowel. "I wasn't doing anything."

He touched her arm. She wouldn't look at him. "Beth? It's all right to accept a compliment." Snyder obviously hadn't given her enough of them.

The reminder of his talk with the guy brought a pang of guilt. He should have discussed it with Beth first, although the conversation had been an impulsive decision, again atypical.

"I have to set the table now," she said, her gaze still averted.

"First, I have something to tell you."

She finally looked at him, her eyes wary, anxious. She was not going to be happy with what he'd done.

"Never mind. It can wait."

Chapter Seven

"You have to get rid of David on Saturday." Maude had just hung up the phone. "The caterers are coming to take a look at the patio and figure out where else they should set up tables and chairs."

"That shouldn't take long." Beth put the kettle on for some tea, and then dried her hands. "He'll probably work until noon. Can't they come in the morning?"

"We can't take the chance he'll come home early." Maude stared distractedly out the kitchen window toward the bay. "Anyway, I imagine it will take a while. They'll have to determine an alternative area indoors if it's too cold or foggy on the tenth."

Beth had dreaded the fact this day could come. She didn't want to be alone with him for any period of time. Not even a minute. "Why can't they come on a weekday?"

"Time is short. Since Ida refused to help me, I'm behind schedule. It's bad enough I had to pull a few strings to get Gerard's to agree to do the party, I certainly don't want to start dictating when they can come and prepare."

Beth got down the cups and saucers, feeling increasingly uneasy. "Why wouldn't Ida help?"

Maude sniffed. "She thinks David will be angry."

Oh, great. Beth knew Ida had misgivings, but out and out refusing to help made it sound more serious. The last thing Beth needed was David angry with her. He didn't seem too thrilled with her as it was lately. "Doesn't he like parties?"

"He can take them or leave them. But this is different. A fortieth birthday is a milestone."

Beth cleared her throat. "I just don't want to get in any trouble with him."

"Is that what's worrying you?" Maude waved a hand. "You let me take care of David if he gets testy with you. All you have to do is get him to take you for a ride on Saturday."

Beth wasn't reassured. "Won't that make him suspicious?"

"Not if you ask him to go to wine country."

"Wine country?" Beth gave a startled laugh. "That won't make him suspicious?"

"About twice a year David goes to Napa Valley to taste the latest vintage and pick up a few cases of a Merlot and Cabernet he favors. I'll mention that we're low on both, and you'll say that you always wanted to see Napa."

"He won't go for it."

Maude stopped filling the blue china bowl with sugar cubes. "Of course he will. I'll simply suggest he take you along for the ride."

Beth shook her head. "He probably enjoys making the trip alone."

"Nonsense. It's a three-hour trip one way. He doesn't need all that time to worry about work. He does enough of that already."

"Three hours?" Beth sank onto a chair, trying to picture six hours in a car with David. That was so not going to happen. She'd never make it without putting her foot in her mouth. "Round-trip would take all day."

"Actually, he spends the night at a hotel and comes home early the next morning."

Beth gaped at her. "I can't spend the night with him."

Maude's eyebrows arched in amusement. "Not literally, I suppose. Although I can't imagine it wouldn't do him some good."

Beth's cheeks got so hot she thought they'd explode. She got up and busied herself with the whistling kettle. "You know what I mean."

"Don't worry. I'll be sure to instruct him you'll need two rooms."

"Why wine country?" Beth asked, ignoring the glint of teasing in the other woman's eyes. "Why can't we go someplace closer, like Fisherman's Wharf?"

"If you can think of a reason to get him to go there, then by all means…"

Beth heard the garage door opening. Again, David was home earlier than expected. For a man who supposedly liked routine, he sure was unpredictable. He claimed he was tired. Maude just smiled. Beth figured he was worried that she'd rip off the family silver.

"This is precisely my point." Maude sighed. "We

can't take the chance that he'll suddenly pop up on Saturday. You'll have to get rid of him.''

The kitchen door opened and both women quieted. David looked a little startled coming through the door, obviously not expecting them to be standing there and staring at him.

He looked from one to the other, his gaze narrowing. ''What are you two up to?''

''Nothing,'' Beth said quickly.

''We're having tea.'' Maude gestured to the set table. ''Care to join us?''

He looked unconvinced. ''No, thank you. I have work to do.''

''Really, David, coming home early because you're tired and then burying yourself in your office makes no sense. Come sit with us.''

The wary look he slid Beth was not her imagination. She grabbed the tin of cookies Maude had with her tea and set them on a plate. ''I think I'll skip tea today. I have to get ready for Mr. Ito's lesson.''

''You have plenty of time. Sit.'' Maude pointed to the white leather kitchen chair. She truly was a wonderful woman, but she was definitely used to having her way and made no bones about it.

Beth obeyed, sinking slowly onto the chair, carefully avoiding David's gaze.

''David, you, too.'' Maude pointed to the chair beside Beth.

He snorted, but set down his briefcase. Then he loosened his tie, slipped off his jacket and laid them both over the unoccupied chair. ''One cup.''

Someone could've knocked Beth over with a

feather. Maude looked pretty surprised, too, but she smiled with satisfaction and poured the tea.

After too long a silence, David reached for his brief-case. "Before I forget—"

Maude groaned. "Can't we have a nice cup of tea without you dragging business into it? I refuse to sign anything until after dinner."

He gave her a tolerant smile. "This has nothing to do with the firm." He snapped open the briefcase and withdrew a book. "This is for you."

Beth stared at the thick hardback he handed her.

"I passed a bookstore today and thought that might help you with Mr. Ito." He cleared his throat and turned to Maude. "Have you heard from Ida?"

"Not since Monday." Maude leaned forward for a better look at the cover. "What is it?"

Touched and shocked David had gone out of his way like that, Beth couldn't even give her the simple answer.

"It's a book about teaching and learning English as a second language," David finally said. "I figured it might be helpful."

"How wonderfully thoughtful." Maude's pleased gaze went back to Beth. "That will be perfect reading material for your trip to Napa Valley."

Beth groaned softly.

David frowned at her, the most peculiar panicky look on his face. "You're going to Napa? When?"

"Saturday," Maude said before Beth could even open her mouth. "With you."

CRYSTAL BLUE SKIES, crisp clean air, the day couldn't be more beautiful. David's Jaguar hugged the road with ease, and snuggled in the comfortable bucket seat nearly had Beth dozing only a mile away from the house.

"We'll stop for lunch in a couple of hours," David said, glancing at the dashboard clock.

"We just had breakfast."

"You might need to stop."

"If I do, I'll let you know." She sounded more curt than she intended, and added, "Please don't change your normal routine on my account."

She dragged her gaze back to the scenery. Everything was so lush and green. Even if it weren't, better she kept her attention off David.

He looked especially good today, relaxed and casual in jeans and a light blue polo shirt. He hadn't shaved, which was totally unlike him. Even Maude had given him an odd look. Even odder, she hadn't commented.

Good thing. Beth was having enough trouble acting and sounding normal. She couldn't believe she was actually sitting here alone with him...for three more hours yet. And then of course there was tonight...tomorrow morning. Basically, they were stuck with each other for the next twenty-four hours.

"Oh, hell."

Her gaze flew to him. Had the same thought just occurred to him?

He slid her a wry look. "I forgot you get carsick."

"Will the road get twisty?"

"No, but we'll be going over some hills."

Her hand went protectively to her stomach. "I'll be okay."

"If you want me to stop at any time—"

"I'll tell you," she finished. "Believe me, I won't be shy about it. I'd hate to—" She cut herself off, deciding she needn't be so graphic.

He laughed. "Yeah, I'd hate for you to do that, too. Although these leather seats wash off pretty well."

She so seldom heard him laugh that she couldn't help but stare. He looked so boyish and relaxed. It made her smile.

"What?" He gave her a double take.

"You laughed."

He squinted at her. "And?"

"I like it." She gave her head a shake. "I mean, it makes you seem relaxed, and I'm glad. You work hard."

The corner of his mouth lifted a little. "I like what I do, so it doesn't seem hard to me."

"You're very lucky."

"Was that a wistful sigh I heard?" He didn't look at her but concentrated on taking a curve in the road. "You won't have to cook for other people for long."

"I don't mind that at all. Some day I hope to be cooking for a whole houseful." She noticed the way his expression tightened, and she looked out the window again. "I only meant that some people live their entire lives not liking their jobs. But they don't do anything about it. They just keep doing what makes them unhappy. It's sad."

Out of the corner of her eye, she saw him give her a quizzical look. For goodness sakes, she hadn't meant to sound so cryptic.

"I'm speaking in general terms," she said. "I'm not talking about myself."

"Ah."

She didn't like the sound of that. Not that she had to prove anything to him. "My brother is one of those people. I honestly don't think he likes farming. Not that I blame him one bit. But he won't make the break."

"Sounds like you didn't like farming either."

"I didn't." She thought back on the night she'd told Junior she was leaving. They'd had an awful fight. Their first real blowout. "That's one of the reasons I left."

"The other was Snyder, I take it."

"Partially. I'd gone as far as I could at the local community college. I had to find another school to finish my degree."

But she hadn't finished. She hadn't even enrolled. Tommy had talked her into waiting so that they could use her college money. She tried to remember what David might have overheard that night she'd had it out with Tommy. She really didn't want to talk about dropping out of school. That she'd been so gullible still shamed her.

"Which was?"

It took her a moment to get back on track. "Home Economics. I want to teach."

His brows rose. "No wonder I've gained five pounds since you've been with us. You're a terrific cook."

Pleasure warmed her to the tips of her toes. "You

haven't tasted anything yet. I've tried to be conservative."

He gave her a crooked grin that made her heart sputter. "Feel free to experiment. I eat anything. And since Mother eats like a bird, we won't worry about her."

Beth laughed. What a heady experience to be sitting here with him in such a light mood. The trip was definitely looking up. "I could cook all day and it wouldn't bother me."

"Maybe you should go to a culinary arts school." He darted her a glance. "For the credentials, not because you need it."

She grinned. "Knock it off or my head will grow too big to get out of the car."

He smiled and returned his attention to the road. They traveled the next ten miles or so without speaking again. Beth didn't mind. She'd always been comfortable with silence. Life on a farm was far from social, except for the occasional community picnic or county fair.

They met with some road construction and while David focused solely on his driving, she used the opportunity to watch him. It was hard to reconcile the man she knew with the one Tommy had described. She didn't fool herself that David could be a tough boss. He demanded excellence from himself, of course he would expect the best from those who represented his firm.

But she knew he was also fair and compassionate. Not just because he'd taken her in, given her a home and a job for the next few months, but by the way he treated Ida and his mother. But most of all, the book he'd given Beth…the mere reminder took her breath away.

They came to a stop behind a string of cars while a cement truck crossed the road in front of them. Down to one lane, they had to wait for oncoming traffic to pass before they could continue.

"Tourists and weekenders mostly travel this road." David grimaced when a small rock skimmed his windshield. "Why they'd have the work crews out on a Saturday is beyond me."

Beth hid a smile. It was nice that even when David was annoyed he could hold onto his temper. Tommy would be cussing a blue streak and flipping off the construction workers. No telling what Junior would have done. Probably would've gotten out of the car and got himself into a whole lot of trouble.

"They probably did work all week, but have a deadline coming up. Plus, sometimes bonuses are involved for the construction company to get done early. The sooner they finish, the larger the bonus. The amount decreases as they get closer to the contracted completion date." Beth thought for a moment. "Of course these are probably county workers."

He gave her a funny look.

"What?"

"How do you know about that?"

She shrugged. "I just do."

"Well, you're right."

"You don't have to sound so surprised. I'm not a hick."

"The thought never crossed my mind. It's just that's not the usual topic of conversation for—what?"

She glared. "Go ahead, say it."

"What?"

"For someone so young. That's what you were going to say, right?"

He lifted a shoulder. "Something like that."

"Why do you always have to point out how young I am?"

He sighed. "That wasn't my intention."

"Twenty-four—I mean, twenty-five isn't that young, and besides, I've always been precocious for my age."

He smiled. "I bet."

"I'm serious. I skipped second and seventh grades. Since I was a late-in-life-baby, my brother is twelve years older and my parents were already in their midforties when I was born. So other than my school friends, who were usually older because of the grade skipping, I always hung around older people."

"What happened to your parents?"

"They died in a car accident when I was fifteen. My brother took over my guardianship, but basically I handled all the household duties from shopping to cooking to cleaning. He was busy trying to work the farm."

"Tough childhood."

"Not really. I loved to read and had lots of time to do it."

"You still read?"

She grinned. "I already made quite a dent in your library."

"I've read most everything in there. We'll have to compare notes."

"You're on."

He smiled at her and then looked back to the road, and hit the brakes. "What the hell—?"

Half on, half off the road, a large tan sedan was stalled. At first, Beth couldn't see any occupants. But then she noticed a man bent near the back rear tire. He straightened when he heard them, although he was so short he'd be easy to miss. His lined face was beaded with perspiration, and his balding head had already started to turn red from the sun.

"You're going to stop, aren't you?"

"Of course." David was already coasting to a stop behind the car.

They had turned off the main highway a couple of miles back and no other cars were on the road. The older man looked more than a little relieved to see them.

"Stay here," David said as he opened his door. "I'll find out what's going on."

"Nonsense." Beth's imitation of Maude was perfect and even David laughed, although he didn't seem pleased that Beth wasn't willing to stay put.

Too bad. She got out along with him and met the stranded man halfway. Near the car under a shade tree, a woman stood, fanning herself. Her plump face was flushed and glistening with perspiration. It wasn't really hot but they both had on conservative churchgoing clothes.

"I'm glad to see you two," the man said, wiping the sweat from his forehead with a white handkerchief. "We've been here near an hour without seeing a soul."

"Did you break down, or have you got a flat?" David went around the side of the car.

"A flat."

"Thank goodness," Beth said and both men looked at her as if she were crazy. A flat was at least manageable. "I'm Beth, and this is David."

"I'm afraid I can't shake your hand. Mine are too grimy, but I'm Arthur Corn. That's my wife Mildred over there."

The woman hobbled toward them. Like her husband, she was at least seventy, as plump as he was lean. She had on an old-fashioned, blue-veiled hat and white gloves. It was her white pumps that obviously gave her difficulty walking on the uneven ground.

"What kind of road service do you have?" David asked, and the couple exchanged concerned glances. "Triple A, or maybe something through your insurance carrier."

"I'm afraid we don't belong to any service." Arthur gave his wife a sheepish look. "We had to cut some corners earlier this year. Guess that was the wrong one to cut."

"No problem. I can get mine to do it." David unfastened his cell phone from his belt.

The woman touched her husband's arm. "We'll be late for Rhonda's wedding."

He patted her hand. "She'll understand."

Beth walked around the side of the car that had the flat. It was a plain old garden-variety flat tire. No wheel or rim damage.

"What a day for this to happen," Mildred said, coming up alongside Beth and shaking her head at the tire. "My sister's grandchild is the one getting married. That old biddy is going to think we were late on purpose." Mildred glanced at Beth. "My sister, not Rhonda. Rhonda is a sweet potato. Mamie's a pain in the fanny."

Beth laughed. "Every family has one." She bent down to get a better look. "Do you have a spare?"

"Yes, but I couldn't allow Arthur to change it. He had a heart attack last year and he's not supposed to exert himself."

"No, of course not." Beth stood, dusted her hands and looked over the trunk at David. "But there's no reason David and I can't change it."

Murder gleamed in his eyes.

Chapter Eight

"Oh, my goodness gracious, we wouldn't want to put you out." Mildred's eyes lit with hope.

Great, just great. David tried to keep his expression neutral. Just because he wanted to wring Beth's neck didn't mean he had to make the other two uncomfortable.

"It won't take us but half an hour." Beth darted him a nervous look, and pushed up her sleeves.

He crooked his finger at her. "May I speak with you a minute?"

"Sure." She smiled at the older couple and then followed him a short distance away.

"We don't want to cause you two any trouble," Arthur called after them.

"No trouble," Beth said, and then faced David and in a low voice asked, "Right?"

"Wrong. I'll be happy to call my service, but we aren't going to change the tire."

"How long do you think it would take someone to get out here?"

"I have no idea."

"They'll miss the wedding."

David sighed. "Look, I'll tell the dispatcher there's an extra fifty in it for someone to get out here within an hour."

She shook her head, her mouth set in a firm line. "That's too long. We can have them on the road much sooner."

"We aren't going to change the tire."

"Why not?"

He groaned. She wouldn't give in. He hadn't seen this stubborn side to her before, but it was evident in the way she lifted her chin and held his gaze.

"Because we can't," he said firmly.

"That was a mature answer."

"Beth, I'm serious."

"Fine." She pushed her sleeves further back. "I'll do it."

He caught her arm before she turned away. "I don't know how to change one. Happy?"

Surprise flickered across her face. "It's easy."

"Anything is easy when you know how to do it." His temper had sparked but he did his best to keep it under wraps. What the hell difference did it make whether he knew how to change a tire or not? There were people trained and paid to do that sort of thing.

"I'll show you," she said softly, her eyes wide and searching. "Or I can do it and you can just help with the heavy stuff."

He briefly closed his eyes and sighed. It wouldn't kill him to give it a try. "I'm going to regret this."

She grinned. "No, you won't."

She grabbed his hand and tugged him back toward the car. The touch was innocent and friendly, but it did a number on his equilibrium. Her palm was warm and soft, and inspired a longing in him that sent up a dozen red flags.

What would she do if he pressed that palm to his bare chest? Or dragged it down his belly? Or cupped it to…

He pulled out of her grasp, took in a deep breath, and then turned away from the hurt look she gave him. Of all days for his mind to get on that track. Mixed feelings about staying in Napa for the night had plagued him all week. He'd been tempted to return to San Francisco this evening. But God only knew what his mother would make of that deviation from the norm.

"Arthur, Mildred said you have a spare tire. I sure hope you have a jack to go along with it." Beth had taken charge.

She stood near the trunk waiting for Arthur to open it, and virtually ignored David. He let her take out the jack but stepped in to remove the spare tire. From there he followed her lead. She obviously knew what she was doing as if she'd done it a dozen times before, and to his amazement, they completed the task in less than half an hour.

"You're both angels," Mildred said, as they stowed the jack and damaged tire in the trunk. She'd sat in the Jag with the air conditioner on and she looked a lot better, not so flushed. "I don't know what we would have done without you."

"I'm glad we could help." Beth rubbed her palms down the front of her jeans, sending David's wayward thoughts back into a tailspin. "Now, you'd better get a move on if you want to make it to that wedding."

"You're right. Arthur..." Mildred nudged her husband with an elbow.

"Don't worry, Dear, I'll take care of it." The older man extended a hand to David, and chuckled. "It's clean now."

David glanced down at his own dirt-streaked hand and kept it to himself. "Wish I could say the same."

Arthur would have none of his reluctance. He grabbed David's hand and pumped it hard. "Thank you, son. Can't tell you how much we appreciate your help."

When the man withdrew, David felt something pressed to his palm. He glanced down as Arthur said goodbye to Beth. It was a five-dollar bill.

David stared at it. He tried not to seem obvious but he was so shocked and not a little overwhelmed by the gesture. His gaze slid to Beth. It didn't appear she'd noticed. What the hell was he going to do? He couldn't keep the money.

"I hate to seem rude, but we'd better get going if we want to see the bride walk down the aisle." Her goodbyes said, Mildred went around to the passenger door.

Arthur shrugged as he turned toward the car, and muttered, "I didn't want to go in the first place."

"Wait."

Everyone looked at David. Too bad he didn't know what to say. "I, uh, I noticed a cooler on your back seat. Could I trouble you for something to drink?"

"Of course." Mildred sighed and reached for the

back door handle. "I'm so sorry we didn't think to offer you some."

Beth opened her mouth and he shot her a warning look. She frowned, but got the message and said nothing. He knew she'd packed some Evian for them.

"You two go ahead and get in the car," David said, hurrying to open the back door. "I'll just grab something and you can be off."

"There are colas and water and small cans of orange juice. Sometimes Arthur's blood sugar drops and—"

"Get in the car, Mildred. They don't need to hear about my blood sugar." Arthur rolled his eyes and climbed in behind the wheel.

"Don't forget to get one for Beth," Mildred said as she got in.

David didn't know how he could get his wallet out of his pocket without being observed. Beth was the one he had to worry about, but there wasn't much he could do about that.

As inconspicuously as possible, he slid his wallet out of his back pocket, pulled out a couple of hundred-dollar bills, added it to the five and threw them in the cooler on top of a loaf of bread. He almost forgot to grab a cola.

He didn't know how much Beth had seen but he ignored her and got back in the Jag. She waited until the older couple had safely pulled onto the road before she got in.

Her mile-wide smile told him she'd seen enough. "That was so nice, I could just kiss you."

David started the car, trying not to react, telling

himself that was only a figure of speech. He didn't want to have a discussion, either. The deed was done…the subject was closed. Period. He reached to turn up the volume for the radio.

Beth stopped him with a hand on his wrist. "They'll probably be madder than a couple of hornets when they find the money, but I'm sure they could use it. Thank you."

"You don't have to thank me."

"I know."

He eyed her hand still on his wrist. "Do you mind?"

She let go, and then turned off the radio.

His gaze went to her face. She was still smiling. "I was listening to that."

"Tough."

He snorted with disbelief. "Tough?"

"You just don't want to hear how wonderful I think you are."

Oh, brother. "Look, that car is old. They may have more trouble with it. That's all."

"I see." She lowered her voice to a gruff teasing.

"End of story." He sent her a look that sent most of the people in his office running in the opposite direction.

Beth laughed. "You're a softie and you don't want me to know. Too late."

"May I listen to the radio now?"

"That depends. What do you want to listen to?"

He sighed. "Not big band music if that's what you're worried about."

"Huh?"

Great. She hadn't even heard of that music era. "It's the type of music they had back in the forties and fifties."

"I know that. In fact, I won a dance contest once to the sounds of Guy Lombardo. What I don't understand is why you'd think I wouldn't want to listen to that kind of music."

He slid her a sideways glance to see if she was serious. Her wrinkled nose drew attention to the faint scattering of freckles across the bridge. She looked twelve. If one person mistook her for his daughter, he'd deck them.

"Now, if you wanted to listen to talk radio," she said. "I'd have to put in my two cents. I hate that stuff. Especially the political topics."

David smiled. "You're safe. No talk radio for me either."

"What's your favorite music?"

He thought for a minute. "Classic rock. And I do mean classic. Nothing beats the Stones, the Doors, Bob Seger back in the late sixties and seventies. But I also like classical music…Bach…Beethoven… Chopin."

"I like all of that, too, but I also like jazz and reggae."

"Really?" Interesting. He would never have guessed.

"Yup. In fact, I like every kind of music."

"Even rap?"

"*That* isn't music."

He chuckled. "You aren't shy of opinions."

"I have another."

Her baiting tone gave him pause. "Opinion?"

"Oh, my gosh, we have to stop."

They were on the verge of passing a small store on the side of the road. David made a sharp right and pulled off the road. The sign hanging from the eaves of the roof boasted freshly roasted nuts, but he supposed they had a restroom.

He pulled the Jag into a small dirt parking lot in the front. The place almost looked deserted. No other cars were parked there, but a red sign on the door indicated it was open for business.

"Aren't you coming in?" Beth asked as she started to get out while he made no move.

"I'll wait here."

"Then I'll just surprise you."

She'd already surprised him plenty. "What?"

"Either you come in with me, or you eat whatever kind I get."

"You're going to buy nuts?"

She gave him a dry look, and then glanced at the sign. "No, I was hoping they had hammers and nails for sale."

"I thought you needed a restroom," he muttered, annoyed that she'd made him stop for something so frivolous.

"What I need are cashews and pistachios. And hopefully they have chocolate. Nothing, and I do mean nothing, goes better with cashews."

At the excitement in her face his irritation ebbed. Grudgingly he got out of the car. No point in waiting out here in the heat. God only knew how long she'd take.

She gave him a big smile that brought his annoyance down another notch, and then hurried ahead of him inside the shop.

The place was old but well kept, the wooden porch floor swept clean beneath a hand carved redwood bench. Amazing craftsmanship detailed the legs and rolled top. He paused for a closer look. On the back were two sets of carved initials and a date. It looked like eighteen hundred and something.

Funny, he'd made this trip to Napa at least fifty times and he'd never noticed this store before. Of course there had been no reason to. Leave it to Beth to sidetrack them.

She was already chatting with someone stooped behind a narrow counter when he entered. Two big barrels of peanuts and pistachios sat side by side near the front window. Along the wall a long table was covered with an assortment of already packaged nuts.

"We have both almond and cashew brittle, too, if you're interested." A stocky blond man, probably in his late-sixties, straightened, and laid something on the counter. "My wife makes it but her arthritis has been acting up so we don't have too large a selection right now." The man nodded to David. "Mornin'."

Beth turned to him. "Do you like brittle?"

"I don't think I've ever had any."

She rolled her eyes and then turned back to the man. "We'll take one of each, please. And a jar of the honey also. David, would you mind scooping some pistachios? They're in the barrel." She handed him a white paper sack.

"How much?"

She frowned. "Better fill it up."

It was a pretty big bag. But he didn't want to have to stop on the way back either. He did as she asked while she browsed through the already packaged goods. She had quite a pile of goodies by the time he brought the pistachios to the counter.

"Hungry?"

She laughed. "Some of it will be for cooking. I have a couple of recipes I've been dying to try."

"We have raw cashews if you'd like." The man weighed the pistachios and punched the price into a calculator. "Anything else?"

"Hmm…" Beth glanced around, as if making sure she hadn't forgotten anything. "I think this will do it."

"With this sale, I can close up shop for the rest of the day." The man chuckled as he continued inputting figures in the calculator.

David reached into his back pocket for his wallet when he thought he smelled cinnamon. He sniffed the air. Cinnamon and chocolate.

A door in the back of the store opened and a woman appeared carrying a tray of steaming mugs. "I thought I heard guests." She had one of those infectious smiles even though her gray eyes looked tired. "I just made some hot chocolate if anyone's interested."

The man abandoned the calculator and hurried to take the tray from her. "Bonnie, you shouldn't be carrying this."

"Oh, stop. I'm fine. Have some chocolate, everyone."

Glancing at his watch, David was tempted to pass,

but the aroma was really getting to him. On nippy winter mornings or when he was home sick from school, his mother used to make him hot chocolate with cinnamon and nutmeg. The unexpected nostalgia had him reaching for one of the mugs.

"Thank you," he said. "It smells terrific."

Beth hadn't moved and he slid her a curious look. She was watching him, an odd expression on her face.

"Ma'am, would you like some?" Bonnie asked her, and Beth turned her attention to the woman.

"Yes, thank you. You shouldn't have gone to the trouble but David is right. It smells heavenly. And I'm Beth, by the way."

"No, you shouldn't have gone to the trouble." The man gave Bonnie an admonishing look, and then sent David and Beth an apologetic one. "Her arthritis causes her a lot of pain."

David took another look at the woman. She seemed too young to be his wife or have arthritis. But then she waved a dismissive hand at her husband, and David sucked in a breath at the damning evidence of the disease.

Her left hand and fingers were bent and distorted. How she'd even managed the tray David couldn't fathom. Her right hand seemed all right at least. Her smile said she made the best of life.

David said nothing while the two women chatted about recipes and the man finished calculating their total. Beth asked to use the restroom and Bonnie took her through the back door. When the tape was finished, David opened his wallet.

The older man ignored him and went on to package the bags of nuts not already in the brown grocery sack.

"What's the damage?" David finally asked when the guy looked as if he weren't in any hurry to get paid.

He shook his head. "Your wife said I wasn't to take any money from you. She's paying."

David drew his head back in surprise. "She's not my wife and I am paying. How much?"

"But she said—"

"How much?"

The man scratched his head, darted a look toward the doorway.

David used the opportunity to grab the receipt, glanced at it, and then laid three bills on the counter. "Keep the change, and please thank your wife for the hot chocolate."

He pulled his keys out of his pocket and picked up the brown bag. He didn't bother asking the guy to tell Beth he'd be in the car. She'd figure it out.

He got in the Jag and waited another five minutes before she came out of the store with a long face. She got in the passenger side, folded her arms across her chest and made a sound of disgust.

"You had no business paying for my purchases."

"Didn't you say you were going to try out recipes?" He backed the car out onto the road. "That comes under household expenses."

"Don't split hairs."

"Come on, Beth, it was only a few bucks."

She reached into her purse. "How much?"

"Break me off a piece of that almond brittle, would you?"

"Nice try. How much?"

"I'd hate to have to do it while I'm driving."

She muttered something under her breath and then twisted around to get to the package on the back seat. It was in the corner behind her and she had to get on her knees to reach it. David slowed down since she'd taken off her seat belt.

The angle of her body gave him an excellent view of her nicely rounded backside. When she stretched for the bag, her fanny ended up inches from his face and he nearly swerved off the road. The sudden jolt sent her leaning into him, her lush bottom pressing against his shoulder.

She instantly righted herself, twisted round and sunk back into her seat. "What happened?"

"Sorry. My fault."

"Was it a deer?" She looked into the side mirror. Woods stretched behind them for miles.

"Yeah."

"Well, at least you didn't hit the poor critter." She started to reach around to the back seat again.

"Wait until we stop. You need to keep your seat belt on." They'd pull over soon enough. He needed a cold drink. Better yet, an ice-cold shower. His concentration was shot. All he could think about was the round softness of her backside.

"Okay," she said slowly. "Now, how much?"

"How much what?" He sent her a quick frown and then returned his eyes to the road. It was beginning to twist and turn some.

"The nuts."

"Jeez, you have a one-track mind."

"Yup, how much?"

"We'll discuss it later."

"There's nothing to discuss." She paused. "How would you feel if the situation were reversed? Would you let someone else pay your way? Do you know how hard it is for me to accept you and your mother's charity?"

"Charity, hell. You're earning your keep."

"Yeah, but—"

"No 'yeah buts.' You're filling in for Ida. You're not window dressing, Beth. You wouldn't know how to be. You're doing a great job. Mother is happy with you." He hadn't meant to sound so harsh, but she didn't give herself enough credit. "*I'm* happy with you."

"Thank you. I'm glad I'm filling a need. Now, how much were the nuts?"

David chuckled and shook his head. She gave *stubborn* a new name. "Ten dollars."

"No way."

"I got a discount."

"David."

"You asked…I told you."

She stewed in silence for a moment and then dug into her purse and pulled out a ten-dollar bill. She laid it on the console between them. "Makes me wonder what else you've lied about," she muttered.

He smiled at her dig. And then he remembered his talk with Tom Snyder. David hadn't said anything to her about it yet. Was he ever not looking forward to that confession.

Chapter Nine

Beth insisted on buying lunch when they stopped at a funky new age café about forty miles from the hotel where they'd be staying. She was both surprised and pleased that David hadn't balked when she suggested they try the vegetarian restaurant. He studied the menu carefully, asked the waitress questions about the preparation and ingredients of two dishes Beth would never have dreamed would've interested him, and then he ordered both.

"Want to try some of this Kung Pao tofu?" he asked. "It's pretty good."

"Isn't it spicy?"

A slow sly smile curved his mouth—one she hadn't seen before. "Not too bad. Might as well give the little guy an eclectic palate right off the bat."

It took her a few seconds to realize he was talking about the baby. He hadn't once referred to her condition since the night he'd taken her home. For whatever reason, the acknowledgement pleased her. "What do you mean 'little guy'? I'm hoping for a girl."

He shook his head as if the matter were settled. "You have to have a boy first."

She laughed. "And this is according to which law?"

"Nature. The boy will always protect his little sister."

"It's obvious you're an only child."

"The minor rivalry doesn't count. In general, a boy will look after his sister."

"That is not always a good thing. Trust me." She stirred her Thai iced tea, and then took a sip of the sweet milky drink. Home should be a haven, a sanctuary, a place of refuge. Junior would make it a living hell if she returned. All because he wanted to protect her.

"Will you tell your brother about the baby?" he asked quietly as if reading her mind.

"Eventually I'll have to."

He stared at her a moment, simmering curiosity in his dark eyes, and then he focused on his food.

She set down her drink. "You want to ask me something."

"Yes, but I don't want to ruin the rest of the day."

She had a feeling she knew what it was. "No 'yeah buts,' remember?"

One side of his mouth lifted. "Have you decided what you're going to do with the baby?"

"No decision was involved. I'm keeping her. I never for a second thought otherwise."

"I figured." He picked up his fork and stabbed a piece of tofu, but not before she saw the approval in his eyes. "I still think you should try some of this."

"Only if you try my couscous salad."

To her surprise he reached over, spooned up some

of the mixture and tasted it. "Not bad, but it needs more mint."

"You've had it before?"

He smiled. "No."

"Con artist."

"Everybody needs a hobby." He pushed his plate toward her. "Your turn."

She studied the chunks of tofu and chose one without any pepper seeds on it. "Hmm, I like it."

"Try some of the vegetables."

Again she studied the assortment of baby corn and straw mushrooms and carrots.

"Would you like me to bring an extra plate?" The redheaded, multi-pierced waitress smiled when Beth looked up. "So that you and your husband can share entrees?"

Beth's gaze slid to David's expressionless face. "I'm just about done." She couldn't resist. "What about you, honey?"

His brows shot up. He quickly swallowed what he had in his mouth. "No, thanks."

Beth smiled at the waitress, trying her darndest not to burst out laughing at his flabbergasted face. "Thanks, but we'll just take the check."

As soon as the woman walked away, Beth didn't hold back. She laughed until tears filled her eyes.

David grunted. "It wasn't that funny."

"You didn't see your face." A thought struck her and she sobered. "Did I embarrass you?"

"Of course not." His voice lacked conviction.

She looked down at her faded jeans and discount T-shirt, and suddenly wished she'd worn one of the spiffy outfits Maude bought her. But for car traveling she'd figured the jeans were good enough. Sadness tightened her chest. A man like David wouldn't have a wife who looked like this.

"Excuse me, I've got to go to the ladies' room." She started to get up but he caught her wrist.

"Wait." He tugged gently, and to avoid a scene, she sank back into her chair. "I apparently said something wrong." He released his grasp but let his hand cover hers as it lay limply on the table.

His touch was warm and reassuring, much like a caress, and her pulse sped up. The ridiculous urge to turn her hand over so that their palms met left her a little shaky. What a way to make things worse between them.

She shook her head. "No, it was me. I wasn't thinking."

"Want to let me in on it?"

She stared down at the bowl of couscous. It turned her stomach. "I shouldn't have let the waitress think I was your wife looking like this."

"Like what?"

She plucked meaningfully at her T-shirt…as if he weren't playing dumb.

His brows drew together and he looked as stern as she'd ever seen him. "I hope you're not implying what I think you are."

Mutely she stared at him, not sure what to say.

"If I showed any reaction at all, it was out of concern that it looks as though I've…" He paused. "…robbed the cradle, as they say."

Beth could only gape at him. "You're serious."

He said nothing while the waitress laid down the check, and removed their plates. When she'd left he said, "Bad enough you're only twenty-five, you look twelve."

"So?" She absolutely did not look twelve, but she'd save that argument for later.

"So, we hardly look like a couple."

"Gee, that's funny. Two sets of strangers thought otherwise today. Not that I want to look like your wife," she added quickly. "But I'm sick of you pointing out how young I look."

His ignored her comment, picked up the check and pulled out his wallet.

"Hey, I said I was paying for lunch." She tried to snatch the bill out of his hand without success.

"I didn't agree to that. You're here with me as an employee. This is business. I'm paying."

"An employee?" Beth rarely lost her temper, but she was close now.

He wouldn't look up, but concentrated on flipping through a wad of cash. Then he put it with the check on the tray the waitress had left. "Ready?"

She grabbed her purse and got up. The restaurant was crowded with mismatched tables and rattan chairs, leaving only a narrow path to the door. She wove her way to the front aware that he was right behind her.

It was those crazy hormones again, she figured, making her unreasonably annoyed with him. What did it matter what he thought? After all, he was *only* her employer.

Darn it. He sure didn't always act like just her employer. She hadn't imagined the heated looks he occasionally gave her, or the touches that weren't strictly casual. And then there was that evening in his den.

The more she thought about that night, the more she realized sparks had flown from both sides. Okay, maybe she was the one who'd kissed his cheek, but he hadn't exactly backed out of harm's way. The thing was, she still thought about it a lot, and wondered what it would be like to kiss David. Really kiss him. Not a crummy peck on the cheek.

"Beth, wait up."

About to push through the door, she glanced over her shoulder, and saw that he'd gotten detoured by a couple of toddlers playing musical chairs at their table. Every time he tried to step around them, they'd move into his way again. He didn't get angry, though, but simply tried to sidestep them. When he finally broke away, he ruffled the little girl's hair, making her giggle.

The scene warmed Beth to her core. Tommy had never been patient with children. And as much as she adored Junior, he wasn't exactly the model father. He yelled too much when he got annoyed with the two littlest ones.

"You took your sweet time," she said teasing, when he joined her outside the café.

"Look, what I said back there..." He sighed, and lifted his hand in a helpless gesture. "I didn't mean to sound impersonal. Of course you're not just an employee."

She knew that, although it had taken her a while to figure things out. The pieces hadn't started to fit together until this morning when every time awareness flared between them, David pointed out how young she was.

She tilted her head back to look at him, squinting a little to protect her eyes from the sun. They were close. He didn't attempt to move away. "But I am."

He shook his head, staring back, his eyes intense, probing. "You know better."

She held on to his gaze. "If I'm not just an employee, then what am I?"

He blinked and his gaze shifted to the young couple passing by on the sidewalk. Was he searching for words? Figuring out how he could deny there was something beginning to blossom between them? Or maybe she was totally off base. Maybe he was thinking of a way to cushion her feelings because he flat-out wasn't interested.

No, she wasn't that stupid or naïve. There were signs...

Weren't there?

David cleared his throat. "I guess I think of you more as a companion to Mother."

That smarted even though it was mostly true. "A paid companion. That makes me an employee. I rest my case, counselor."

"Beth, come on." He followed her to the car, and then stood there, dangling his keys in the air, when she tried to open the locked door.

"Are you going to let me in?"

"Eventually...after you listen."

"Okay." She folded her arms across her chest.

His gaze lowered briefly to where the T-shirt fabric strained across her breasts. "You've become a friend to Mother and I both. I think she's always wanted a daughter, and in a way, you're filling that need for her.''

''So, that would also make me the sister you never had, right?''

''Right.'' At least he had the good grace to flinch.

''Bull.''

His left eyebrow went up. ''How eloquent.''

''Go ahead make fun of me, try and distract me all you want. But we both know something else is going on here.''

Something that looked like dread sparked briefly in his eyes. She heard his sharp intake of breath as he glanced around and raked a nervous hand through his hair. ''This isn't the place to have this discussion.''

''No denial?'' A grin tugged at her mouth. ''Well, that's progress.''

''Don't get any ideas.'' He pressed the remote and unlocked the car doors.

''Too late.'' She laughed when he rolled his gaze heavenward, and reached for her door handle. And then he muttered something about the impulsiveness of youth. She stopped, thought a moment.

Impulsive, huh? She'd show him impulsive.

She opened the door, flung her purse onto the passenger seat, and then before he could climb in, went around the hood and threw her arms around his neck. He stumbled back in surprise, his hands going to her waist.

She smiled up at his shocked face. ''How's this for impulsive?''

She kissed him on the mouth, hard and thorough,

until his lips softened in surrender and his hands tightened at her waist. He made a low guttural sound in his throat and what had started out as mockery turned into raw desire. She pressed against him, her tender breasts rubbing his hard chest. When she finally had regained the power to break away, she didn't know which one of them was more shaken.

DAVID SKIPPED checking into the hotel and headed straight to the winery. His lips still burned from Beth's kiss and his heart thudded with the reminder. No way could he check into a room right now and not do something irrevocably foolish. He'd like to think he was bigger than that, more mature, more in control, but he sure as hell wasn't going to take the chance.

There was also the business of changing the reservation. The two-bedroom suite he'd booked wouldn't do. They'd have to share a common area. Not now they couldn't. In fact, he'd have them put her on another floor altogether.

He chanced a glance at her. She stared out at the scenery, acres of terraced vineyards planted mainly in cabernet savignon and chardonnay grapes, oblivious to the fact that she'd just set him on fire.

"What's that huge, old building over there?" she asked, squinting in the direction of the winery. "It looks like a castle."

He was dying, and she was studying old buildings? "That's Martinelli and Son's Winery. We're headed there now."

Her gaze flew to him. "I thought we were going to the hotel first."

"I changed my mind."

"You could have warned me."

He frowned at her snappy tone. So, maybe she wasn't as unaffected as she'd pretended. "I didn't think it mattered."

"Well, it does. I have to use the ladies' room."

"You should have done that back at the restaurant."

"I would have done just that, if you'd warned me weren't going straight to the hotel."

He turned the car down the long, winding drive to the winery, wondering what had made her so prickly. Was she regretting the kiss? Upset by the enthusiastic way he'd reacted? God, what a mess.

They drove the five minutes it took to get there in silence. David knew he'd have to say something eventually. Something ridiculous like, let's pretend the kiss never happened. But now wasn't the time. Not because he was a coward...exactly. When they got to the privacy of the hotel, there'd be time for...

His thoughts went haywire.

Oh, man, he was in trouble.

It was barely noon and the parking lot was already half full. Fortunately they didn't have to wait in any of the tourist lines. They weren't here for the tour, only a tasting and to purchase two cases of wine.

David pulled the car around to the side close to the residence and parked in his usual spot. Beth was still quiet but probably because she seemed interested in the building and vineyards. Good. The distraction was perfect timing. Maybe it wouldn't be a bad idea if she did tour the place. His old friend Roberto would give her a private showing. And David could take the time to recuperate.

He ushered them to a side entrance, which took them to Roberto's office. The door was open and Roberto was on the phone, lounging back in his tall leather chair, his feet, crossed at the ankles, resting on the massive antique desk.

As soon as he saw them he grinned and swung his feet down. He eyed Beth with undisguised interest, motioning for them to sit on the pair of club chairs opposite him. He wound up his conversation in accented English, said his goodbye in Italian and then hung up the phone.

"David, I didn't expect you for another couple of hours," he said, the Italian accent gone, as he stood to shake David's hand. His gaze went to Beth.

"We're ahead of schedule and since I figured you were loafing anyway..."

"Hey." Roberto laughed good-naturedly, and then winked at Beth. "He lies."

"Right." David grunted. "Beth Anderson meet Roberto Martinelli."

Roberto flashed the killer smile that had kept his college nights busy, and came around the desk to take Beth's hand. He brought it to his lips, and captured her gaze. "You have the most remarkable blue eyes. But of course, you hear that all the time."

Beth blushed. "Thank you."

David shook his head. He'd met Roberto in college where he'd done more romancing than studying. Nice guy but you couldn't trust him as far as you could throw him when it came to women. That fact had slipped David's mind.

Until now.

"Okay, Casanova, you have my wine order?"

Roberto released Beth's hand and lifted a dark brow at David. "Why the hurry? I have two Merlots for you to taste—a seventy-four and a sixty-one."

"We've been on the road all morning, and Beth is tired—"

"No, I'm not." She smiled at Roberto. "I'd love to see the inside of the winery if that's okay."

"But of course." Roberto was all teeth.

Beth's mood had sure lifted in a hurry. "I would like to freshen up first."

"Down the hall to the left is the ladies' room. You can't miss it." Roberto gestured with his hand. "Take your time."

She slid David the briefest glance before slipping out the door.

Roberto watched her go. "She's something. Meg Ryan, only sexier." His gaze went to David. "Not your usual type."

"I didn't know I had one. Anyway, she's only a friend...of Mother's and mine."

"Ah." Roberto's interested gaze returned toward the door even though Beth was gone.

David cursed to himself. He knew that predatory look. What an idiot he'd been to practically declare Beth open season. But it was none of his business. She was a big girl, or so she reminded him often enough. She could take care of herself.

"What about these two Merlots?" he asked his

friend, promptly distracting him. Easy enough. Wine was another of Roberto's passions.

"I have a vintage that will make you weep." Roberto kissed his pursed fingertips. "Primo stuff. Unfortunately it won't be ready until your next trip. However, I do have a cabernet that we will uncork today. How about staying for lunch?"

"We just finished, but I wouldn't be averse to some tastings."

"Good. As soon as Beth..." Roberto's eyes lit up as he looked past David. "Ah, here she is."

David turned and immediately saw that she'd put on lipstick. It was a pale pink shade but he was certain he would have noticed it before had she been wearing any. Of course it was no big deal....

"We were just discussing a private tasting of our recent vintage," Roberto said, taking her by the arm. "After that, perhaps you'd like a private tour of the winery and vineyards."

"On second thought, I'm not sure we have time." They both looked at him with puzzled frowns. "I was thinking about heading up to Healdsburg in the morning and then swinging by Bodega Bay on the way back down to the city."

Roberto made a dismissive sound. "Why?"

"Beth hasn't seen that part of the state." He darted her a look. She stared at him with open curiosity.

"That's tomorrow," Roberto said, smiling at Beth. "We have all afternoon."

David shook his head. "We've got to hit Glen Ellen Winery for my mother. We'll have to do that next."

"Are you staying only one night?" Roberto asked,

and when David nodded, he said, "You're cramming a lot into one trip."

David shrugged. "I'm trying to give Beth an abbreviated tour." He glanced at his watch, and then at Beth. "And if you're interested in seeing Jack London State Historic Park after Glen Ellen, we've got to get going."

That got her attention. "I'd love to."

Roberto grunted. "What's there to see? London's house burned down before he could even move in."

Her attention went to David. "London actually lived near here?"

"He wrote all his Alaskan wilderness and open sea stories right here in Sonoma. He owned fourteen-hundred acres of forest. That's where he had Wolf House built, on a bluff overlooking the Valley of the Moon. But as Roberto said, it burned to the ground. I believe there's not much left but a stonewall. Still, it's only a short hike and a beautiful view."

"I vote we go see it," she said, moving away from Roberto.

David smiled. He had her. Now, what the hell was he going to do with her?

Chapter Ten

Beth wandered around the tasting room with the rest of the tourists while David tried a couple of Merlots and a Chardonnay in a small private room off to the side. She'd thought about taking the tiniest of sips, enough to taste but not enough to hurt the baby, but she decided against it when she realized her motive was strictly to impress David. To appear more sophisticated and worldly, when in truth, she'd only had wine once before and hated the taste.

As much as a tour of the winery appealed to her, visiting Jack London State Historic Park was more enticing. Even if there wasn't much to see, she loved the outdoors and next to spending the time with David, the lush landscape was the best part of the trip.

Now, if only she could concentrate and really enjoy the scenery. And quit thinking about that smack she'd laid on him. Or the way he'd responded by pulling her against him, teasing her lips with his tongue. The mere memory made her warm and tingly and she headed for the small cups of water they had set out.

Not that she was sorry she'd kissed him. Well, maybe a little, but only because the tension between them had grown like dandelions in an open field. Still, she was sick of his remarks about age, or more to the point, how young she was.

She meandered back into the private room and watched David sip the sample Roberto gave him, his head tilted back, his throat working, the sheer bliss on his face as he lowered the crystal glass.

And darn if she didn't get turned on.

As much as she hated to keep blaming her shift in hormones, there was no accounting for her reaction. The man had only taken a drink, for goodness sake, and heat crawled from her tightened nipples, down her belly into her nether region.

She quickly turned away but not before Roberto saw her and motioned for her to join them. He was a good-looking guy, stunning really, with his dark hair and olive skin, teeth so white it blinded you. But he was so transparent it was almost comical. A charmer, a womanizer, a man who likely got what he wanted.

Two months ago she would have been flattered by his compliments and attention. But her experience with Tommy had taught her not to accept anything at face value anymore. She'd been too trusting and naïve. He'd taught her cynicism. She probably ought to thank him. So why did the lesson feel so awful?

She shook away the destructive thoughts and reluctantly approached the men. To do anything else would have been rude.

"Come, Beth, you must taste this." Roberto poured a small amount of wine into a crystal goblet and held it out to her.

She shot David a helpless glance. "I'm not much

of a wine drinker,'' she said, not anxious to announce her condition.

"Ah, but this is not mere wine. It's nirvana.''

David took the goblet out of Roberto's hand and gave her a sympathetic wink. "Sorry, you know you can't have alcohol with the medication you're taking.''

"You're right.'' She nodded, grateful for his quick thinking. She smiled at Roberto. "Next time.''

"Is that a promise to return, lovely lady?'' He took her hand again, kissing the back, leveling his gaze with hers and giving her a meaningful look.

"Possibly,'' she said with a teasing lilt.

"Soon?'' He held on to her hand, using his thumb to brush the underside of her wrist.

With her free hand, she gently rubbed her tummy. "Probably after the baby is born.''

The shock in his eyes and the way he dropped her hand as if he'd just been scorched was worth the loss of her privacy. She smiled brightly at him, heard David cough, and did all she could not to burst out laughing.

Speechless, Roberto looked to David.

"We'd better go,'' he said, and Beth pressed her lips together when she saw the amusement tugging at his mouth. "I assume the two cases of wine have already been loaded in the Jag.''

"Of course.'' Roberto sent David a speculative frown, and then smiled crookedly at Beth. "Nice having met you, and…'' He shrugged. "Congratulations.''

"Thank you,'' she murmured, not feeling so smug anymore. She hadn't meant to implicate David, yet the look Roberto gave him clearly indicated the seed had been planted.

"See you in a few months," David said, and took Beth's arm.

He seemed perfectly okay, but as they left the winery she said, "I'm sorry if Roberto thought that the baby—well, you know. It just that he was being such a flirt, I couldn't resist."

One side of David's mouth hiked up. "That's all right. I'm getting used to your impulsiveness."

She sighed. That jab she couldn't dispute.

They got to the car and he opened her door. "We go to Glen Ellen next."

"And then Jack London Park?"

"Right."

"When are we checking into the hotel?"

"It doesn't matter how late we get there. We have a guaranteed reservation."

Eager as she was to see more of the sights, it seemed odd that he was so ready to abandon his original plan. Especially since he'd warned her before they left San Francisco that the trip would be brief. Suddenly he was ready to take side jaunts. It didn't make sense...

She blinked, as a thought struck her.

Maybe he was putting off going to the hotel. She'd scared him with the kiss, and now he was worried about what might happen once they checked in. A giggle bubbled in her chest.

"How far is it?" she asked casually.

"The hotel?" He glanced away from the road long

enough to see her nod. "From here, or to Glen Ellen?"

"Either."

"I'd guess it's about midpoint. We'll pass it on the way. Why?"

"Then there'd no problem stopping, right?"

He frowned but kept his eyes on the road. "What for?"

"I'd like to freshen up."

"You already did that at Matinelli's."

She chuckled. "That was merely a euphemism for having to use the john. Now I really want to freshen up."

He gave her that look. The one that said he was surprised she knew the word euphemism. Was that ever annoying. That and the fact he didn't say anything, but returned his attention to the road, ignoring her.

"Well, will you stop or not?"

"We won't be that long at Glen Ellen."

"Fine, but that didn't answer my question."

"Check-in isn't until three."

"Only if the room isn't available." She doubted he'd ever had to wait for a check-in time in his life.

"This is a busy weekend because of the hot air balloon festival starting tomorrow. I assure you the suite won't be available yet."

"If you give me your cell phone, I'll call and check."

He grunted. "Why are you being so stubborn?"

"Funny, I was thinking the same thing about you."

Without warning, he veered the car off the side of

the road and parked. "I'll call. I need to check on something anyway."

"I'm perfectly capable of—"

Before she could finish, he got out of the car, taking the phone with him.

Beth stared as he paced to the edge of the woods, out of earshot, as if he had some big secret to hide. Had she really spooked him that badly? Or was something else going on? Maybe he wasn't really calling the hotel. Maybe he had a date with someone he knew who lived out here.

The sudden thought stopped her. That was entirely possible. Maybe that's why he liked to take these trips alone. But of course, he wouldn't have to hide anything like that. Unless the woman was married. No, David wasn't the type to see a married woman.

He was simply calling the hotel, just like he said. But then again, he'd known the number to whomever he called. If he were really calling the hotel, wouldn't he have had to look it up?

Oh, brother. Beth briefly closed her eyes. Her thoughts were really going bonkers now. *She* was going bonkers. Talk about swift payback for being so mischievous.

He finished the call and got back into the car. "Everything is set. We'll stop if you want. Or I can drop you off, and you can rest while I run over to Glen Ellen and get Mother's wine."

She shrugged. "If you have somewhere else to go..."

"You're the one who was so hot to stop at the hotel. I thought you were tired."

Not normally a pouter, Beth said nothing but stared ahead at the road. He was still annoyed with her for the kiss. Well, it wasn't as if she could take it back, for heaven's sake.

He sighed loudly. "What's wrong now?"

"Nothing."

"Right."

"I'm trying to think, okay?"

His left eyebrow went up but he kept his focus straight ahead. Obviously they were getting close to another winery or town. Traffic had picked up.

"Look," she said finally, "don't feel like you have to entertain me. Since you usually come out here alone, you probably have friends you'd like to see, or something else you'd normally do."

"A quiet dinner, a nice bottle of wine and my brief-case—that's my usual routine." He paused. "On the other hand, don't feel as though you have to hang around with me this evening. There are a lot of restaurants and clubs for young people near the hotel."

Amazed, Beth turned to stare at him. "For young people?"

He nodded, without looking at her. The coward. "Your age, the twenties crowd."

"You don't quit, do you?"

He gave her a brief, almost condescending look.

"Maybe there'll be a bingo parlor with forties music in case you get bored," she said sweetly. "Of course that may be a bit too much excitement for someone your age."

David snorted but said nothing.

"If you want to get rid of me tonight, you could

have the decency to be honest and tell me you have other plans or you want to be alone, or whatever.''

"Did I say I wanted to get rid of you?"

"No, that's my point." She stared out the window with a vengeance. She had a good mind to kiss him every time he tried to use age to put distance between them.

The thought sent a shiver down her spine. Kissing him had already gotten her into enough trouble. He was quieter now, more subdued. She'd liked him better on the first leg of the trip.

She'd also liked kissing him. Excitement at the memory fluttered in her chest. Not good. "I wish you'd said something earlier about your date with your briefcase and bottle of wine. Maybe Roberto would have wanted a little company tonight."

David's jaw tightened. "He's not your type."

"That's not what I meant." She sighed. "Men. Sometimes you have one-track minds."

"Knock it off, Beth."

"What?"

"I'm giving you fair warning."

"What on earth are you talking about?"

"You're baiting me and I don't like it."

Beth blinked. He sounded so serious…a little angry even. "And what do you think you've been doing with all the references to 'young people'?"

He steered the car to the right, the turn so sudden she gripped the door handle. They ended up on nothing but a dirt road off the shoulder that disappeared into the woods. He parked the car about a hundred yards from the main road.

She gaped at him when he turned off the engine. "What are you doing?"

Without a word he got out, the expression on his face an odd mix of determination and desperation. He rounded the hood and opened her door. "Out."

She didn't move. "Why?"

"Beth," he said in a low, strained voice. "Get out of the car."

The intensity in his dark eyes would have instilled fear in her had it been anyone but David holding open the door and commanding her to obey him. Instead, curiosity prompted her to slowly swing her legs out of the car, forcing him to back up. He gave her just enough room to stand.

"What are you going to do, leave me here?" she asked, her chin lifted, not entirely sure he wouldn't do just that.

"Don't tempt me."

He swooped down before she knew what was happening, taking her mouth with his, grasping her by the waist and pulling her against him. Startled, she tensed, and then relaxed and slid her arms around his neck.

He tasted of the wine he'd just sampled and his sun-warmed skin smelled clean and rugged like the pine trees that flanked them. His hands moved from her waist to her back, and then lower until her buttocks filled his palms. Heat spiraled through her when the hard length of his arousal nudged her belly.

One light touch of his tongue at the seam of her lips and she opened her eager mouth to him. He slipped inside, exploring every nook and crevice, inviting her tongue to dance, while pulling her body closer with his restless hands.

The kiss wasn't rough or tender, but demanding enough to take the starch out of Beth's knees. This had to be a dream. What else could this slice of ecstasy be? Except his skillful mouth and hands were much better than anything she'd invented as she'd lain in bed at night.

She wound her arms tighter around his neck, pressing closer, looking for relief for her tightened nipples. Her breasts ached for his touch, for the velvet of his tongue. If only they weren't standing in the middle of...

A loud horn honk and a series of catcalls from a passing pickup truck finally forced them apart. Beth took a step back but David's obvious reluctance to release her started that flutter in her chest again.

She hesitated raising her gaze afraid of the hunger he could surely see in her eyes. But when she finally did, his slow sexy smile erased any misgivings.

And then he frowned and gently touched her chin, the corner of her mouth. When he lowered his head again, she held her breath. He lightly kissed the places he'd touched, and then used his tongue to soothe and moisten.

Beth's eyes drifted closed. When she opened them again, he was staring at her, the tenderness in his gaze nearly her undoing. "I'm sorry about the beard burns," he said quietly, cradling her jaw with one large hand. "I forgot I hadn't shaved yet."

"That's okay." Her voice sounded feeble. She

didn't care. Not that she could do anything about it. She was lucky to still be standing.

His hand moved to the back of her neck, kneading, massaging, and making her want to plaster herself against him again. "I shouldn't have done that."

"Kiss me?"

He nodded, his gaze watchful.

"I think I was the one who broke the ice in that department."

He smiled again. But it was a little sad this time. "It's just that you're so—"

"If you say young, I will hurt you."

"I was going to say vulnerable."

"Me?"

"Yes, you."

"Wrong." She took another step back and gave an emphatic shake of her head. "I feel stronger and more in control of my life than ever."

He looked unconvinced. "Even after that business with Snyder?"

"*Especially* after that ordeal with Tommy. Don't you see…I was always under someone's thumb, first my brother, and then Tommy. But when it was time to make the hard decision, I could do it. I left rather than be a victim of Tommy's verbal and emotional abuse."

His brows dipped in a frown. "That doesn't mean you can't be vulnerable. You're pregnant and relying on strangers for food and shelter."

"Strangers?" That smarted, and she grabbed a fistful of his shirt, drew him to her and kissed him hard before letting go. She startled herself as much as him with her audacity but held her ground. "I don't kiss strangers."

"You know what I meant," he said, his voice hoarse. "And don't distract me like that again."

"Or what?"

"So help me, Beth..." His hands clenched at his sides.

She splayed her fingers on his chest. "What?"

"Don't."

She drew back. "Have you ever seen a woman who was really pretty and you couldn't wait to meet her, but as soon as you tried to have a conversation with her, you realized she wasn't anything like you expected?"

"Your point is?"

"I may look young, even vulnerable, but I'm made of steel."

His mouth curved in amusement. "Steel, huh?"

"Okay, maybe aluminum," she said with a grudging smile of her own. "But I'm working up to steel."

"I believe you."

"Wise choice."

"But—"

She put a finger to his lips. "I'm not a child and as much as I appreciate what you and your mother have done for me, I don't feel indebted enough to compromise myself."

He winced slightly.

She swallowed. "I like you, David. I like kissing you. I, um..." She couldn't say it. She couldn't tell him she'd like to do a little more than kissing.

His eyebrows rose in question.

She moved back. "Never mind."

"Yep, aluminum."

"Very funny."

"What were you going to say?"

She moistened her lips, attracting his attention there. Lowering her gaze, she noticed the bulge in his jeans. Her heart skidded. Did she have the nerve? Oh, God, she didn't think so.

"Beth?" He reached for her hand and drew her closer again. "What did you want to say?"

The fronts of their thighs touched. His warm breath skimmed her cheek. No cars were coming from either side of the road. Besides, the Jag effectively blocked anyone's view other than a headshot. It was now or never.

"Beth?" He nudged her chin up. The desire in his eyes gave her courage.

She lowered her free hand and cupped his sex.

Chapter Eleven

David groaned, and she immediately pulled her hand away. He wanted to grab it and bring her warm palm back against his erection, explain that was a moan of pleasure. But he let her go and prayed he didn't embarrass himself.

He couldn't believe she'd actually touched him like that, and judging by her stunned expression, neither could she. Her eyes were bluer than the sky, wide and searching as she took a step back.

"No." He snatched her hand, not wanting her to withdraw from him or be ashamed. He'd practically begged for her touch. None of this was her fault. "Come here."

A small tug and she was in his arms. He held her close, kissed the top of her sun-warmed hair. It was incredibly silky and soft. Just like the rest of her. And her lips…poets wrote about rose petal lips like hers. If he wasn't careful, he could drown in all that softness.

"I can't believe we're standing here like this on the side of the road," she said, tilting her head back to look at him.

He groaned, this time out of exasperation. Granted they were off the beaten path but only insanity would allow for this lapse in good sense. "Let's get out of here."

"Okay." The reluctance in her eyes was endearing.

His gaze helplessly tangled with hers for a moment and he had the ridiculous urge to drag her into the woods and make love to her until the sun went down.

Her sudden shy smile brought him to his senses. What little he had left.

He hugged her once more and then they both got back in the Jag. As awkward as a toddler's first step, silence filled the car for the next mile…long enough for regret to fester. David thought about slipping in a Rolling Stones CD, but that was the coward's way.

"Beth—"

"David—"

They both spoke at the same time.

Beth's laugh was nervous. He cleared his throat.

"You first," she said, before he could.

"I hope I haven't made you uncomfortable." He had more to say. The words wouldn't come.

"Not in the least. Did I embarrass you?"

"Of course not." He'd done enough to humiliate himself. He was supposed to be the mature one. Roberto came to mind. David had tried to protect her from the guy. Who would protect her from David? "I just don't want to ruin your trip. Or our relationship, for that matter."

"You haven't." She reached for one of the bags of nuts she'd purchased earlier. "Want a cashew?"

Startled by her nonchalance, he turned to look at

her. Her head was bowed as she studied the contents
of the bag. Her voice may have been calm, but her
hands shook like leaves in the wind.

GLEN ELLEN WINERY was situated just off the Jack
London State Historic Park's access road. Unlike the
castle style Martinelli Winery, Glen Ellen was com-
prised of white clapboard buildings with blue trim.
Nothing outstanding about them, except for the gar-
dens and strutting peacocks that wandered throughout
the shrubs and flowers.

Until she'd spotted the exotic creatures, Beth had
paid little attention to the scenery. Her pulse rate
hadn't returned to normal, and just thinking about the
kiss and David sent her blood pressure soaring higher
than the bright pink hot air balloon they'd passed a
mile or so back.

"They have sparkling grape juice, if you'd care for
some," David said as they entered the tasting room.

His tone was formal and stiff and her heart plum-
meted. She had a good mind to take a possessive hold
of his arm, but the truth was, she didn't know what
she wanted or expected of him. Maybe it was best that
he was trying to put some distance between them. She
just didn't know.

"I think I'll go find some water."

"Here." He gestured to a water cooler and then
filled a paper cup for her.

"Thanks," she muttered, realizing she could use a
time-out herself. Of course she could always go to the
bathroom again.

David sent her a speculative look but said nothing.

He accepted the sample of wine a young man handed him, sniffed it and then took a sip. He didn't look overly impressed but he smiled at the attendant, and then ushered her toward the next table.

He bowed his head, bringing his lips close to her ear and whispered, "What do you say we grab Mother's wine and get out of here?"

Whether it was his warm breath on her skin or the quiet urgency in his voice that sent her pulse racing over the speed limit, she didn't know, but she nodded and tried not to trip over her feet.

The staff was friendly and David seemed to know most of them but he didn't linger even when one particularly persistent tall, blond woman tried to engage him in conversation. He simply gave his order, and asked that the case of sauvignon blanc be placed in the trunk as he paid the bill.

That Beth caught a few curious stares told her they knew him well enough to be inquisitive about her. But he never introduced her even once and she wasn't sure what to think about that. Of course, he did seem in a hurry.

To get to the hotel?

Oh, God.

One minute she couldn't wait to get there herself, and the next moment the thought scared her witless. She was fairly certain that any further intimacy would have to be initiated by her. He obviously was trying to hold back. Probably reminding himself she was too young.

The idea chafed, but it also meant she'd have to take the bull by the horns…so to speak. The thing was, did she have the guts? Was it even the right thing to do? Her body had no qualms, but she had to consider her vulnerable situation. If she upset him, he could throw her out of this house.

No, he wouldn't do that. Not David. But a misstep could make life pretty uncomfortable for both of them. Could she afford to take that risk?

"You look awfully grim all of a sudden." David held the door open, and she walked out into the sunlight.

"I was just thinking."

His left brow went up.

Yeah, fat chance she'd tell him anything. She kept walking toward the car, staying a step ahead of him and breathing in the crisp, clean air, hoping to clear her head. Only midafternoon and it already had cooled considerably. She shivered slightly, mostly from the nip in the air but also a little from nerves.

As she got to the passenger side, she heard the click of the lock disengaging, and hurried to get inside before David opened the door for her. Silly maybe, but she didn't want any possible physical contact messing up her head again.

David got in and inserted the key into the ignition. "Everything okay?" he asked, his gaze narrowed on her.

"Just fine."

He didn't start the car right away and she braced herself for an inquisition. But after a long moment's silence, he started the engine.

Neither one said anything for the next ten miles. Beth saw the sign for Jack London Historic State Park a minute after they left the winery but she decided against pointing it out. David obviously had a different agenda and she was anxious for it to play out.

"Are there any stops you want to make before we go to the hotel?" he finally asked.

"Such as?"

He shrugged. "I don't know. Just asking."

"Since I'm not familiar with the area, I really don't know," she said when he sounded a little defensive.

"How about a grocery store, drugstore, that sort of thing?" He glanced over at her. "How's your cashew and chocolate stash? Must be dwindling by now."

She looked down at the bag in her lap. The sack of cashews was nearly gone. Had she really eaten that many? She heard his soft chuckle and sent him a wry look. "You had some, too."

"I know." He smiled, but lucky for him he didn't point out that he'd only had a handful. "So, do we need to make a stop?"

She thought for a moment.

"There's a drugstore near the hotel, too."

Odd. That was the second time he'd brought up a drugstore. Why would she want to—? Her breath caught. *Condoms*. Maybe he was hinting they needed condoms. Her mind went blank. Her mouth got so dry she couldn't have spoken even if she could have thought of something to say.

"Toothbrush, toothpaste?" He darted her an inquiring and totally innocent look before returning his attention to the road.

Had she gone insane? How had she taken the leap to condoms? "Got them both."

"Cold cream?"

"What?" She laughed. That was a term she hadn't heard in a while.

"You know what I mean."

"I'm covered in that department."

He steered the car off the main highway onto a narrower two-lane road. Up ahead was a cluster of buildings. As they got closer, he said, "I'm going to have to make a quick stop at the drugstore."

Her gaze went to his profile. He stayed focused on the road. "Forgot something?"

He nodded, but his suddenly clenched jaw made her breath catch again.

Maybe he really was stopping for condoms. Silently, she cleared her throat. "Anything I can help you with?"

He half smiled. "It's personal."

"Oh."

"Deodorant." He shook his head. "What a thing to forget."

Beth swallowed her disappointment. There was no law that said *she* couldn't buy a package of condoms. Not that she knew a blessed thing about them. Tommy had always taken care of that. But how hard could it be?

He pulled the car into a parking stall in front of a large glass window filled with displays and advertised specials. Hanging from the eaves was a sign—Wilbur's Pharmacy.

Oh, no. How could she buy condoms from someone named Wilbur? He was probably a kindly old man, someone's grandfather who would have a coronary if she asked him for condoms.

She rubbed her tummy. The cashews were rebelling. Or maybe it was just nerves.

David cut the engine. "You think of anything you need?"

She shook her head. "I'll wait here."

He seemed relieved, which spurred her suspicion. He left the key in the ignition with an old Beatles' song playing on the radio. "I'll only be a minute."

"I'm in no hurry," she said, getting deceptively comfortable in the leather bucket seat, and then watched and waited until he entered the store.

Even as she tried to talk herself out of it, she knew what she was going to do. She had to indulge herself. It wasn't a simple matter of being nosy. A girl had to be prepared, after all.

As soon as she was confident he was busy with his shopping, she slipped out of the car, remembering at the last minute to take the keys with her. Pretending to study one of the ads in the front window, she peered inside between the signs. The sun's glare made it impossible to see clearly without getting up close to the glass. She walked casually to the far end of the storefront, hoping for a better angle.

A short older woman was at the register. A row behind her, Beth could see the top of David's dark head. At least she thought it was him since no one else appeared to be in the store.

She studied the display of teeth whitening products and then the ad for the antacids the store had on special, while looking for a better view inside. So busy sticking her nose between signs, she almost didn't hear the bell above the door when it opened.

She made an abrupt turn toward the window from the adjoining store.

"Beth? What are you doing?"

She glanced back at him. He had a small white bag in his hand. "Just browsing. I want to get your mom a souvenir."

His narrowed gaze went to the store window where she'd been so studiously focused. "At a maternity shop?"

Beth blinked, and turned back to the display she had yet to notice. An antique-looking cradle had been fashioned from redwood. Tiny, ornate figures of angels were carved into the headboard. Its understated beauty took her breath away.

David came to stand beside her. "Quite a piece of workmanship."

There were other things on display, a high chair, two strollers, a crib, but she knew he meant the cradle. It was incredible. Like something in a fancy magazine. Had generations of tiny babies laid their heads between the polished redwood? "Is it new, do you think, and just made to look antique?"

"One way to find out." He moved to the door, opened it. "Come on."

"Oh, no." She stepped back. "It doesn't matter, really."

His mouth curved in a slow smile. "You can't tell me you aren't interested in having a look around."

"Well…" She shrugged, her gaze going back to the crib and high chair, both handmade, as well. And obviously expensive. Way beyond her means. Heck, a Goodwill thrift store was beyond her means these days. "It's really a waste of time."

"Good thing we have plenty of it." He held the door wider.

She was tempted, all right. Even though it was totally ridiculous to look at anything she couldn't afford. But there were other baby things in the store that she could see through the window, small, more affordable items, and excitement started to churn in her belly. She hadn't done any baby-stuff shopping yet, not even to just browse. Once she knew for sure she was pregnant, everything had happened so fast. Surely there'd be no harm in just looking.

He stood aside as she approached the door and let her go in before him. Having to pass him so closely, being able to feel his heat, inhale his musky scent, made her warm and tingly. Maybe stopping to do a little shopping wasn't such a bad idea. What else would they do once they got to the hotel? The possibilities made her shiver.

She glanced at the white bag still in his hand. Maybe he'd put it down somewhere and she could take a peek. She sighed to herself. Of course she wouldn't do that.

"Good afternoon." A woman came from the back of the store, carrying a large box marked "rattles." Tall, trim and graying, she had a wide pleasant smile. "Anything I can help you with?"

"We're just looking."

"We have a question about the redwood cradle in the window," David said at the same time.

"Ah, you have good taste." The woman set the box on the counter near an old cash register. It had to be over thirty years old. "My name is Merly, by the way. I own the shop."

"I'm David. This is Beth." He put a hand on her lower back.

It wasn't a big deal. Just a friendly, comfortable gesture as they all walked toward the window, except he didn't pull away. He kept his palm pressed against her in a possessive manner. Beth didn't mind. It just surprised the heck out of her.

Merly smiled and eyed Beth's tummy. "First one?"

Beth nodded and glanced down. Was she starting to show more? Excitement and panic tangled, making her chest tight. Sometimes when she laid in the dark at night she had to convince herself she was really pregnant. That is wasn't a dream. It was too easy to forget that nothing had changed. That she'd be going back to school next fall just as she'd planned...that her life wasn't a complete mess.

"Oh, honey, don't look so sad." Merly patted her arm. "The waiting part is far worse than any of the rest of it. You'll see."

Heat stung Beth's cheeks. She couldn't even think of a proper denial.

"I think the problem is too many cashews," David said, slipping an arm around her shoulders and giving her a squeeze. When she slanted him a wry look, he winked.

Merly laughed as she removed a waist-high partition separating the window display from the store. "So the cravings have started already. I drove my husband crazy with all four of my children.''

''Please don't go to any trouble.'' Beth placed a restraining hand on the partition. ''We're just curious about the cradle.''

''Ah, but if you see the fine craftsmanship up close you won't be able to resist.'' The woman cleared the way and gestured for them to get a closer look.

Beth hung back, afraid to get the woman's hope up for a sale. For that matter, Beth wasn't keen on being teased with something she couldn't have either.

David had no such qualms. He stepped up to the cradle, ran a hand over the polished wood. ''When was this made?''

''Around nineteen hundred as best we can determine. It belonged to my neighbor's grandmother. Her husband carved it for their first child. They went on to have six more. Every one of those babies slept in this cradle.''

''It's beautiful. I'm surprised they're willing to let it leave the family,'' Beth said, moving a little closer to see the tiny cherub carved into the center of the headboard.

''Gertie never had any children. Since she was an only child, she didn't have anyone to pass it on to. I told her she might as well see what we could get for it.'' Merly frowned, her interested gaze wandering out toward the Jag. ''That doesn't mean we're willing to let it go cheap. Social Security doesn't go far these days.''

''Regardless of Social Security, this is a fine piece. You should expect a fine price. That said...'' David's lips twisted in a self-deprecating smile. "How much is it?"

"David." Beth tugged at his arm. They both looked at her. "It doesn't matter," she mumbled, wishing Merly was out of earshot. "We should go."

"Would you like some coffee or something? I just made it fresh." Merly had already started toward the back. "Of course you should have orange juice," she said to Beth. "No caffeine. Back in the fifties we didn't know any better and I used to chug that stuff down. I ended up with a hyperactive child that kept me on my toes for eighteen years."

Beth met David's eyes and they exchanged grins. The minor shared intimacy gave her a warm fuzzy. She almost forgot she was annoyed with him.

"David, please don't lead that poor woman on. I can't afford the cradle. I'm not buying it. So what's the point of all this?"

"Do you like it?"

"It doesn't matter."

"Then you shouldn't mind answering."

She let out an exasperated sigh. "Of course I like it. Who wouldn't? It's beautiful. And no, you aren't buying it for me."

His brows went up. "Who said I was?"

"Nobody," she looked away, embarrassed. "I threw that in just in case."

"Perhaps I have another pregnant friend."

Her gaze flew back to him. "Right."

"That would be so unbelievable?"

"Merly's coming." Great. Beth had accomplished nothing in the woman's absence. Maybe she ought to leave him to discuss the cradle and walk over to the pharmacy.

Her gaze lowered to the bag he hadn't released. What the heck was in there?

"Coffee for you." Merly handed David a mug. "And OJ for you," she said to Beth, who hated orange juice with a passion.

"Thank you." She accepted the glass and took a small sip. Nasty stuff. Real, whole oranges were another story.

"Oh, my, I didn't ask if you wanted cream and sugar."

"Black is fine," David said.

"I can't stomach it black." Merly gave an emphatic shake of her head. "My husband, God rest his soul, he liked it so strong and black it tasted bitter to me. So I kept dumping in more cream and sugar so I wouldn't have to make a separate pot."

The woman was lonely, Beth realized. She probably had few customers and no one to talk to all day. It would serve David right if she talked his ear off.

"What's the matter? Why aren't you drinking your orange juice? It's good for you." Merly had certainly gotten familiar fast.

But she was right, and Beth took another dutiful sip. Knowing it was good for her and the baby didn't make the stuff go down any easier. She tried not to cringe.

"I practically lived on orange juice early on with my third pregnancy. And then when I couldn't keep that down, I went to saltines and ginger ale." Merly shook her head, apparently having forgotten about the cradle, or the fact that they were strangers. She gave

David a knowing look. "You'll be running to the store for all sorts of things at all hours. Be prepared."

His smile was patient. His eyes weren't. "About the cradle?"

"Let's see." Merly's face creased as she stared at the cradle. "I want to quote a fair price. How about—?"

The phone rang.

Merly looked at the Donald Duck clock hanging over the door. "That's my son. Excuse me."

Another reprieve. So it wouldn't be a total waste of Merly's time, Beth picked up a couple of bibs and a yellow rattle. They were inexpensive and within reaching distance. Then she looked for a place to set her half full glass. The juice was making her a little queasy.

"What are you doing?" David watched, a frown pulling his brows together.

"I'm going to leave some money for these things, and then wait in the car."

"I'm sure she won't be long."

"Probably not, but then she'll have to repeat her entire phone conversation, and then editorialize." Beth smiled as she pulled out some cash. She didn't mean to sound unkind. Merly reminded her of a chatty great-aunt whom Beth loved to pieces. But she did hope the thought of suffering through a replay discouraged him. "Have fun."

"Wait."

She stopped near the door, but not because he'd asked. Something wasn't right. Her stomach rolled. The bitter taste of orange juice filled her mouth.

Panic consumed her. Oh, God, she thought she might throw up. Not here. Not now.

''Beth?''

Her head got a little light and she grabbed the back of a high chair. She lost her grip of the bibs and her purse. David clamped a hand around her wrist. She slumped against him.

The last thing she saw was the room spinning around like a carousel.

Chapter Twelve

"Beth!" David let out an unexpected curse that made Merly come running.

"What's wrong? Has she fainted?" The older woman helped him settle Beth on a nearby chair.

He stared at her pale face as her head lolled to the side. Her closed eyelids fluttered slightly.

"Beth, can you hear me?"

No response.

"Has she been having trouble with the pregnancy?" Merly asked as she pressed her palm against Beth's forehead.

David swallowed. "I don't think so."

Merly gave him a funny look. "I'll go get a cold compress." She patted him on the shoulder. "Don't worry. I'm sure she'll be fine. The first one is always hard."

He hung on to her reassurance and used it to fend the fear that coiled in his gut. "Beth?"

Again, no response.

He brushed the dark blond hair away from her face, and her eyelids fluttered. Her eyes made a couple of false starts at opening.

"Here, put this across her forehead." Merly handed him a folded damp piece of terry cloth.

He knew she was trying to help, but he wished she'd disappear so he could be alone with Beth. After brushing her bangs aside, he placed the cool compress on her skin. Her eyes finally opened.

He smiled. "Hi."

She blinked. "What happened?"

"You got bored and decided to take a nap."

The corners of her mouth twitched. And then she frowned and shivered.

Panic seized him again. "What?"

"I can still taste that orange juice."

Hovering nearby, Merly sighed. "Honey, you should have said something. I could have given you something else."

Utterly confused, David looked up. "Orange juice caused this?"

Merly shrugged. "Sometimes while you're pregnant you react strangely to different tastes and smells. Even foods you're normally fond of can seem repulsive."

Fascinated, David wanted to ask more questions, but Beth tried to sit up on her own and his attention immediately went back to her. "Why don't you stay still for a while?"

"Because I'm fine. Really." She removed the compress and sat up straight.

Amazingly, she did look okay. Color had returned to her cheeks, her eyes were alert, and a shy smile was beginning to curve her lips.

"What did I tell you?" Merly handed him a filled glass. "She's starting to look good as new."

"What's this?"

"Plain old water."

"Thanks, but I think I'll pass," Beth said. "Nothing is going in my mouth until I get to the hotel."

"Actually, I thought your husband could use it." Merly chuckled. "When he couldn't get you to respond, he looked worse than you did."

Beth stared at him with wide surprised eyes so blue they mesmerized him.

He shrugged. "You scared the hell out of me."

Her lips lifted in a pleased smile. "I did?"

"Of course," he muttered gruffly. "Wouldn't you have been worried if I suddenly took a nosedive?"

"I did no such thing."

"That's because I caught you."

"Oh."

He was still holding her with one arm, one of his knees bent, the other in a kneeling position so that he was nearly eye level with her. The sudden urge to kiss her nearly sent him off balance. Of course he wouldn't be such a jerk. Not now when she wasn't feeling so hot.

Merly cleared her throat. "Can't I get either of you anything?"

David snapped out of his preoccupation. "No, thank you." He stood, but stuck close in case Beth had a problem getting up. "Are you ready to head to the hotel, or do you want to sit a while longer?"

"I'm not trying to rush you," Merly said quickly. "Stay as long as you want. Frankly, I've enjoyed the company. We don't get enough traffic around here since the highway opened."

"I'd really like to get settled in the hotel." Beth pushed to her feet, accepting David's hand when he offered it. Her palm was a little clammy but her grip was firm.

"I don't blame you a bit." Merly took the glass from David. "When I had my second boy, I had to stay off my feet for days at a time. I just watched soap operas and went to the bathroom."

David forced a smile. He knew the woman meant well but she was starting to drive him nuts. If he had to listen to one more of her pregnancy stories, he'd have to stick a pacifier in her mouth.

On the one hand he wanted to ask a dozen questions, on the other it frustrated him to realize how ignorant he was of the entire pregnancy process. How much did Beth know? Maybe if he bought a couple of books...

"David?" Beth's soft voice cut into his thoughts. "Would you mind?"

He followed her gaze and saw that the rattles and bibs she'd picked out were scattered on the floor. He scooped them up, and then reached for his wallet.

She put a hand on his arm. "I already left some money for them." She glanced at Merly. "Over there on the counter where the bibs and diaper bags are displayed. It's five dollars over so that should cover the tax."

Merly looked puzzled. "Do you want a bag or a receipt?"

"No, that's okay." Beth stopped, a chagrined expression on her face. "I haven't even thanked you."

"Oh, my goodness." Merly waved a hand. "I

didn't do a thing. You just worry about getting some rest and taking care of yourself. When you feel better, maybe you'll still want that cradle.''

David had forgotten all about that. Judging by the startled look on Beth's face, so had she. Before he could respond, he felt a tug at his hand.

''I'd really like to get going,'' she said, giving him a persuasive smile.

''Of course.'' He turned to Merly. ''Thanks for all your help. Perhaps I'll see you later.''

He opened the door for Beth, ignoring her disapproving frown, and immediately used the remote to unlock the Jag. If she didn't like the idea of him buying the cradle, then that was tough. It was for the baby, not her.

They'd gotten to the car and he'd opened the passenger door when Merly called out from the shop door for him to wait.

''You forgot this,'' she said, holding up the white sack with his pharmacy purchase.

While Beth got into the car, he went back to get the bag. Merly didn't immediately let go. Their eyes met.

''Please, please don't worry,'' she said, ''but try to keep your wife's stress level down. I'm sure it's nothing that she got light-headed, but it is early in the pregnancy, and stress can be such a debilitating factor.''

Don't worry? Right. ''Thanks.''

Merly stopped him with a hand on his arm. ''You look dreadful. I'm afraid I've done more harm than good. There's really nothing to worry about, I'm sure.''

He nodded, but she couldn't be certain. Neither could he. He wondered how long it had been since Beth had seen a doctor. He had a good mind to drive directly back to San Francisco right now. It would be evening by the time they got back but he had no doubt he could find a doctor to see her. But then again, maybe a good night's rest before the long drive would be better.

She looked at him with a strange expression on her face, and he started to panic, but then realized he was standing in front of the Jag, staring off into space like an idiot. No wonder she gave him a funny look.

He quickly got behind the wheel and tucked the white paper sack under his seat. It seemed he wouldn't be needing it, after all.

BETH HAD NEVER in her life been in such a ritzy hotel. She hated to look like a gawking tourist but she couldn't help staring at the huge mosaic fountain in the center of the lobby, or the brass sculptures of a man and a woman on either side of the long mahogany reception desk.

An assistant manager had come out to greet David as though he were some kind of royalty. She hung back even though David tried to include her. The whole experience was really weird, sort of intimidating.

"Are you all right?" he whispered in her ear when the young man went behind the reception desk to get their keys.

"I'm fine."

"You don't look it."

"If I'm acting strange, it has nothing to do with my health. You may be used to all this attention, I'm not."

He frowned as though he didn't understand.

"When you gave your name to the valet parker, I thought the poor guy was going to hurt himself hurrying to let his supervisor know you were here."

David sighed. "It's a hotel. I'm a repeat guest. They're practicing good P.R."

"I bet if I came back twice a year for the next five years in a row they wouldn't treat me like that."

He made a face. "I guess you are fine."

"I told you I was." She smiled. "It was nice that you were worried about me, though."

"When was the last time you saw the doctor?" He didn't smile back, but looked awfully serious.

She shrugged. "To confirm I was pregnant."

"Shouldn't you be seeing him more regularly?"

"Her. And no, it's not time for me to go back yet."

"Because you didn't have health insurance?"

"What are you, my father?" she snapped without thinking, and then covered her mouth with her hand, and mumbled, "I'm sorry."

His lips thinned, and his face tightened.

She glanced around. The lobby wasn't crowded, and anyway, no one paid them any attention. "I'm taking the proper vitamins. I don't have to go back for a while. I wouldn't jeopardize the baby because I didn't have health insurance."

He gave a curt nod.

Why couldn't she have said that in the first place? Hadn't she just told him it was nice that he'd been worried about her? "Look, I'm really sorry I snapped."

"Forget it."

"But you've been so nice—" She stopped when the assistant manager approached, but the look on David's face had been enough to cut her off.

What had she said to make him look so grim? For goodness sakes, she'd only said he was nice. That was a good thing. So why did he look as though she'd insulted him?

"If you'll come with me," the manager was saying, "I'll show you to your suite. Of course the Bell Captain will have your luggage brought right up."

"My bag." Beth twisted around. "I left it in the car."

"They'll take care of it."

"But I just have that one small—"

"Yes, I know." David put his hand at the small of her back. "They'll bring it up shortly."

That one casual touch reduced her to a meek little lamb, and without another word, she followed the manager as he led the way to the elevators.

"Is this your first time with us?" the man asked. He was about her age, maybe a little older, cute with sandy-blond hair and gorgeous dimples.

"Yes. First time in Napa, in fact."

"Ah, then I hope you're staying for a few days. There's so much to see. And what many people don't realize is that we have quite the nightlife if you know where to go. I'd be happy to—" He shot a nervous look at David. "Our concierge can provide you with some options, if you like."

She gave him her best smile. "Thank you, but we're leaving in the morning."

David remained quiet during the elevator ride and all the way to the end of the corridor where they were shown through the richly polished double doors of the President's Suite.

Entering the elegant parlor, Beth gasped, ignoring the sharp looks of both men. Not only was the décor incredible with the glossy hardwood floors, Persian rugs and enormous Oriental urns, but the view from the panoramic glass windows was breathtaking.

Acres of green vineyards and trees starting to turn orange and yellow stretched as far as she could see against a sky that was remarkably blue now that the morning haze had totally burned off. Off to the right a pair of pink and yellow hot air balloons floated toward the sun.

"I trust you approve." The manager smiled. Don, she thought his name was, and stole a look at his nametag to be sure.

"Oh, no, I hate it." They both laughed.

David didn't. What was wrong with him?

"At night there'll be lots of lights from both the vineyards and some of the area's nightspots. And there is no better sunset in the world." Don glanced at David. "Of course since this is your usual suite, you already know this, Mr. Matthews."

"Yes, thank you." David paced to the window but it was obvious he wasn't enjoying the scenery. He seemed edgy, distracted. Was he still worried about her? Or maybe he thought he was stuck baby-sitting her now. "Will the bags be up shortly?"

"They're on their way." Don apparently noticed David's grim mood, as well. He glanced from Beth to David. "Shall I show the lady the rest of the suite?"

"Sure." David gave an absent nod without looking away from the window.

Beth wasn't particularly interested. She wanted to get rid of Don so she could find out what was wrong with David. But since someone would be showing up with their bags anyway, she followed the manager around as he showed her a large Jacuzzi in a bathroom the size of Texas and a wet bar with a fully stocked refrigerator with enough chocolate bars to keep her queasy for a week.

The parlor alone was as large as the apartment she'd shared with Tommy, and then they got to the bedroom. Holy cow. It was big enough to have a king-size bed, a couch and two massive royal blue velveteen chairs that someone could easily sleep on.

Don opened the drapes to the same view as the parlor. "That's an adjoining bedroom," he said, indicating a closed door to the right of the entry. "But of course—"

The doorbell rang, cutting him off.

David was still standing at the window when Don went to the door. A room service waiter rolled in a table set with a silver tray of fresh fruit, a variety of cheeses and a bottle of wine. Behind him another uniformed man brought in a huge bouquet of red carnations, yellow roses and white mums.

"Good afternoon, ma'am. Where would you like this?" the room service waiter asked.

She glanced at David for instructions. He was watching her but said nothing.

Fine. She turned back to the waiter. "How about over here between the window and dining room table?"

"I can transfer everything to the table if you'd like."

Beth thought for a moment. It wasn't like they needed the room. "David, do you have an opinion?"

He shook his head.

She stared back at him for a moment. She didn't think he was trying to be difficult, but he wasn't exactly Mr. Congeniality either.

"Do the balcony doors open?" Beth asked Don.

"Absolutely. You may want to sit out there before it gets too cool."

She smiled at the waiter. "How about you leave everything as is near the window?"

"Yes, ma'am." The man pushed the cart in place and set the brake.

"And the flowers?" the second man asked.

"On the coffee table, please," she said without hesitation. The view was so spectacular from the parlor she knew she'd be spending a lot of time on the couch. With the flowers on the coffee table, she'd be able to enjoy them, as well.

David finally moved away from the window, reached into his pocket for his money clip and handed each man a folded bill. A moment after they'd left, another man showed up with the small overnight bags Beth and David had each brought.

Again, David left her to handle the man and the

logistics of depositing the bags, which irked her a little. He'd never made her feel like an employee before, but she sure felt like his maid or assistant about now. And then she sighed with the sad realization that she was his employee.

She had the bellman leave both bags outside the bedroom she'd just seen not knowing which bedroom was hers. David came around enough to give the man a tip. He was still in an odd mood, though, and Beth was suddenly anxious for Don to leave so that she could find out what was going on.

"Thank you," she said, turning to him, hoping she didn't sound too dismissive or abrupt. She knew where the other bedroom was through the connecting door. That's the only thing he hadn't shown her yet. "You've been very helpful."

"My pleasure." He smiled, not appearing at all put out. "If there's anything else you need, here's my extension." He handed her a card. "Mr. Matthews, it's nice having you with us again."

David frowned when the man moved toward the door. "Do you have a key for me?"

Don darted a confused look at the card keys he'd given Beth and she'd lain on the foyer table. "Didn't I include two?"

"I meant for my room."

The confusion on the manager's face heightened. "These keys open both."

David shook his head. "I arranged for another room down the hall."

Beth shot him a surprised look. It was her understanding they'd share a suite, separate rooms of course. He wouldn't acknowledge her.

Don looked embarrassed. "I'm sorry. I thought your reservation was for a two-bedroom suite. Obviously we've made an error."

"Right, but then earlier today I called and arranged for a second room." David paused, but avoided her gaze. "One not attached to the suite."

"I apologize for the misunderstanding, Mr. Matthews. Excuse me while I call the front desk. I'm sure I can get this straightened out in no time."

Hurt and confused, Beth stared at David. He still wouldn't look at her, but went back to gazing out the window. When had he decided they couldn't share a suite? That was probably the call he'd made earlier when he pulled off to the side of the road. But what had triggered it? The kiss?

She tried to think back on the events right before he'd made the call, but so much had happened this morning. Staring at his somber profile, she was tempted to ask him for an explanation. Did he think she was going to attack him, for heaven's sake? She'd wait until they were alone, though, when he couldn't give her a patronizing answer.

Don hung up the phone, the grim expression on his face telling. "We have a problem."

David turned away from the window, his jaw tight. He said nothing, but only looked at Don until the poor guy started to shift nervously.

"Apparently when you called earlier, the front desk clerk misunderstood your instructions. She said it was difficult to hear because of the static." Don darted

Beth an anxious look. "Of course I realize that's no excuse—"

David held up a hand. "What's the bottom line?"

"The hotel is full. We don't have an extra room. I'm sorry. I don't know what we can do..."

David pushed a hand through his hair and sighed. "Never mind. We'll take these rooms."

Don cleared his throat. "You mean the parlor and the bedroom?"

"I mean, the entire two-bedroom suite."

"That's part of the problem." The poor man looked as though he wanted to seep into the carpet. "The clerk thought you were giving up the second room."

Chapter Thirteen

David forced himself to remain calm. "What do you mean you sold it? I had a guaranteed reservation."

"Yes, sir." The young man glanced at Beth. What? Did he think she was going to help him? "But the clerk thought you said you no longer needed it, and since we were overbooked—"

"Why would she think I didn't need it when I was calling for another room?" Dammit. What a mess! He couldn't even think straight.

"David?" Beth touched his arm but he wouldn't look at her.

He peered at the man's nametag. "Are you the manager on duty?"

"Yes, sir."

"What are you going to do about this?"

"I assure you, sir, if we had an available room, I'd—"

"I'm not interested in your excuses," David said, cutting the man off. "I want a solution."

"David." Beth laid a hand on his arm again, and this time when he wouldn't acknowledge her, she gave a hard tug. He turned and faced her with a frown.

"May I talk with you for a moment?" Her expression and tone were firm. The question was obviously rhetorical.

"Later."

"Now." She smiled sweetly.

He was tempted to ignore her but the determination in her eyes made him think twice. Better to hear her out. "Excuse us, please."

"Certainly." Don disappeared into the next room.

David watched her pace to the window and back again as if trying to organize her thoughts. God only knew what she must be thinking. That he'd purposely given away the extra room and was trying to force her into bed with him. She'd feel helpless, at his mercy, unsure how she could turn him down and not lose a roof over her head. Poor girl...

She stopped and faced him. "You're being an ass."

"I beg your pardon."

"Do you honestly want me to repeat it?"

He stared at her in mute disbelief. She seemed genuinely annoyed with him, and apparently wasn't afraid to show it.

"Someone made a mistake. At least we still have someplace to stay tonight." She narrowed her gaze like a disapproving schoolteacher. "It's not the end of the world."

"That's not the point."

"Okay." She put her hands on her hips, making her T-shirt strain across her breasts. "I'm listening."

"There's only one bedroom."

"For goodness sakes, there's a whole big parlor. I'll sleep on the couch." She walked over and pushed down on the seat cushion with her palm. "Nice and soft. I'll be very comfortable here."

"If it comes to that, I'll sleep on the couch."

She sighed. "It's come to that, David. Go tell Don he's off the hook."

"Is that what this is about? Protecting your new friend in there?"

She looked affronted at first, and then amused. "You sound jealous."

Denial raced through him. "How absurd," he said, his voice lowered. "Why would I—" He shook his head, unwilling to expand the topic. "Go tell him everything is fine. We'll share the suite."

"I promise I won't bite," she whispered as she strolled past, the teasing lilt in her voice goading him.

He snagged her wrist, stopping her, and then with a small tug, forced her back a step. Bringing his lips close to her ear, he said, "I can't make that promise."

ALL THROUGH dinner Beth waited for the other shoe to drop, for David to make a move, or do or say something that would hint at what he had in mind tonight. But he acted so blasé it made her want to scream.

Several times he asked her how she was feeling, if she thought it might be wise to see a local doctor. She knew he meant well, even though he was annoying the heck out of her, so she did her best to assure him she was all right.

"What are we doing after dinner?" she finally asked.

He raised a wary gaze from the credit card voucher he was signing. "Why?"

She snorted. "Why?"

He frowned, his eyes narrowed.

"Because I want to know if you had anything in mind. Why else would I ask?"

A smile lifted one side of his mouth. "Want to take a walk?"

"Where?"

"There's a garden out back."

"What kind of garden?"

He pushed back from the table and then went around to pull out her chair. "Come on."

She stood, and on impulse took his hand. His gaze immediately swept the small intimate dining room. No one even looked up.

As soon as they got outside she asked, "Why did you look around like that?"

"Like what?" He tried to withdraw his hand. She held on tight.

She grinned. "Like you thought everyone might be pointing and laughing."

He grunted and shook his head.

Beth wouldn't be dismissed. "You're the only one who sees the age difference between us."

"Really?" He gave her a very irritating and patronizing look. "And how do you know that?"

"Because everyone assumes we're married, and they don't even bat an eye."

"Everyone, huh?"

"The people with whom we came into contact today. Deny that."

He shook his head again as if she were a pesky child.

They were passing a gift shop and she suddenly pulled him to the door. "Look, honey, look at that porcelain doll. Wouldn't your mother love that for her collection?"

The store clerk had just stepped out from arranging the window display. "We have more inside the store."

David stared at Beth. "What are you talking about?"

"Come on." She winked at him.

His eyebrows drew together in confusion.

"While your wife looks at the dolls, we have a collection of classic model cars that may interest you," the clerk said, the hope of a sale in her smile.

Beth watched realization dawn on his face. She tried not to give him an I-told-you-so look. "Let's go have a look. I really would like to take something back for your mom."

"Tell you what." He lifted her chin with his finger. "You go in, and I'll meet you back here in about fifteen minutes."

It was hard to think with him staring her in the eyes, and then letting his gaze rest on her lips, his hand drifting from her chin to the back of her neck.

He lowered his head and briefly touched her lips with his. "Okay?"

She made a gurgling sound. It was pretty embarrassing. "Okay."

He kissed her again, a little firmer this time but still light enough to only tease her. To her mortification, she felt herself rise on tiptoes for a more satisfying kiss. David complied, and her insides started to flutter.

Thankfully the clerk had gone about her business

and no one else was around, but Beth still felt awfully vulnerable standing half in the doorway and half on the sidewalk. Public displays of affection had always been taboo in the small community of Rock Falls.

She pulled away and cast a quick glance down the sidewalk. A couple was absorbed in window-shopping two stores down.

"What's the matter?" A mocking smile lifted the corners of his mouth. "Afraid people are pointing and laughing?"

She gave him a light jab in the ribs that made him grunt. "Keep it up and I will give them something to talk about."

His look of quiet amusement caught her off guard.

"You don't believe me?" She gave him a haughty lift of her chin. Not that she had the faintest idea what she'd do next.

"I didn't say a word." He glanced at his watch. "I'll be back in fifteen minutes," he said as if the last couple of minutes had never happened, as if he considered her no threat at all.

He really did think she was a child. Well, she'd just have to show him differently. She just had to figure out how the heck to do that.

DAVID HADN'T MEANT to tick off Beth. But he obviously had done a fine job of it. She said nothing the entire walk back to the hotel, or the short trip up the elevator. He'd give just about anything to know what was going on in that pretty head of hers. She was up to something. That was for certain.

Hell, that was about the only thing he did know for

certain. Never in his life had he been so off balance. One minute he convinced himself there could be something between them, and the next minute he was calling himself a fool. All evening he'd been alternating between wanting to hurry back to the suite or club hopping until they were both too drop-dead tired to think about the sleeping arrangements.

The thing was, something about Beth was making an idiot out of him. He'd always enjoyed sex as much as the next guy, but she had him thinking about it at every turn. She'd say or do the most innocent thing and he'd take some giant leap in the direction of them both naked, limbs tangled between the sheets.

In the final analysis, he knew he wouldn't make a move. She wanted protection and shelter, not sex. Besides, she was... Any extracurricular activity couldn't be good for her or the baby. God, he wished he knew more about the pregnancy process.

He opened the door to the suite and then stepped aside to let Beth in first. She briefly eyed the package in his hand before stepping over the threshold.

David hid a smile. He knew she'd been nosy about what he'd bought when he left her at the gift shop, but she stubbornly hadn't asked what it was. Good thing. He wasn't about to tell her.

She walked directly to the flowers, briefly closed her eyes and sniffed before dropping her purse on a console table. The simple blue silk dress she wore suited her coloring perfectly and made her look so slim it was hard to believe she was pregnant.

"What's wrong?" She frowned, the uncertainty in her eyes clear, and he realized he'd been staring.

"I was just thinking how beautiful you look."

Pink instantly flooded her face. "No, really."

Her reaction took him by surprise. Although it shouldn't have. He doubted Snyder paid her many compliments. "Yes, really. You look beautiful."

She turned away, almost unwilling to hear or believe him. And dammit, he didn't know what to do. Pretend nothing had happened? Make her look him in the eyes until she believed him? The answer would be simple if there wasn't a king-size bed in the next room as inconspicuous as an indignant defendant in a courtroom.

"You can use the bathroom first if you like." She kicked off her shoes and went to the wet bar for a bottle of Evian.

"We have two…one in the parlor. But anyway, it's early." Water sounded good. He caught the refrigerator door before she closed it. "Were you planning on going to bed already?"

She jumped.

He took out a bottle for himself. "I didn't mean to startle you."

"Sorry, I should have asked if you wanted one."

"Look, we've had a nice trip so far. Let's not spoil it."

Her gaze flew to his. "How am I spoiling it?"

"I didn't say you were." He took his time untwisting the cap. "But I'm sure you feel the awkwardness as much as I do."

She shrugged, turned toward the window. Outside the lights were rather spectacular. Some of the vineyards strung white lights around their property, making odd patterns throughout the valley. From this height it was quite a display.

Her reflection in the glass captured his interest. The fear and doubt on her face nearly broke his heart. He was pushing too hard and she didn't know how to fend him off without jeopardizing their arrangement. God, he was a jerk.

"I think I'll go for another walk." He set down the bottle of Evian, but before he could even turn toward the door, she spun around.

"Wait." She crossed her arms and hugged herself. "Will you be gone long?"

He shrugged. Long enough for her to lock the bedroom door and get in bed. But he didn't think he should offer that reassurance. It might embarrass her.

She noisily cleared her throat. "Do you have to go?"

He frowned, unsure he understood.

"Are you leaving because of me?" Color climbed her neck and spread through her cheeks. "I'll lay off. I promise."

Now, he was really confused. "Lay off?"

She looked away. "I know I've been pushy."

David thought for a moment, and then started to laugh. She flashed him a look of indignation, and he shook his head. "I'm laughing at me."

Her arms went from crossed to folded in a defensive gesture. She drew in her lower lip, making her look incredibly young.

His bravado faltered, but if he didn't explain she'd imagine the worst. "I'd just been thinking the same thing."

She blinked. "That I'd been too pushy?"

He laughed again. "No, that *I've* been too pushy."

Her brows went up and she dropped her arms to her sides. "That's not true."

The genuine surprise in her face reassured him. "It's sure felt like it to me." He exhaled and rubbed the weariness from behind his neck. "Of course, you don't know what's been running through my head," he muttered to himself.

"Tell me." Her eyes had lit up and she moved a little closer.

He slid her a peeved glance, although his annoyance was self-directed. "That wasn't meant for your ears."

Her lips had started to curve. "Maybe it was a Freudian slip."

"You think so?" He let his gaze run down her body. There was nothing Freudian about what he was doing. He wanted to make her uncomfortable, make her run away. They were treading dangerous water. One of them had to do something to break the current.

She nodded, and took a step closer. "Tell me what's been running through your head."

"Not a good idea."

"Some of history's most successful inventions started with a bad idea." She got up so close that he needed only to lower his head a few inches to kiss her. But she wasn't as confident as she pretended. Her hands shook some, and there was a tiny quiver in her lower lip.

"Beth, we have to be careful, and really think about how our relationship can change forever." He placed his hands on her shoulders.

Big mistake. He'd meant to be comforting, brotherly, but her fragile heat seared his palms, sent a current of desire through him that made him wish to high heaven he was made of stronger stuff than the mush barely holding him together.

He started to jerk away but she covered one of his hands with hers, and lifted herself on tiptoes to brush her lips against his. God help him, but he kissed her back. Not hard, but firmly enough to let her know what a weak excuse for a man he was.

She released his hand and then slid her arms around his neck. His hands automatically fell from her shoulders, and then one of his arms found its way around her waist. She was still so slim for being pregnant...

The reminder was like having someone turn a hose on him. "Beth, you're grateful to me, and I can understand how you might feel—"

"That I have to prostitute myself?" She slackened her arms around his neck and tilted her head back to glare at him with angry eyes.

He splayed his fingers and massaged the small of her back. "You know that's not what I mean."

"That's basically what you're implying."

"No, I'm suggesting that you may be confused."

She edged further away. "I'm not the one who's confused. I know exactly what I want."

God, he wanted to ask what she meant, but like any attorney with half a brain knew, you never asked a question to which you didn't already know the answer. But that was in the courtroom. This was personal. And he was a damn coward.

She took the matter out of his hands by capturing

and holding his gaze, and then saying, "Tell me you have no interest in me, and I'll—I'll—fade into the sunset."

Her dramatic attempt would have been funny at any other time. "Of course I'm interested in you and I don't want you fading off anywhere."

"No, no." She waved an agitated hand. "I know you're interested, but I mean *interested*... as in like a woman, and not just a charity case."

"I never considered you a charity case."

"You know what I mean, and you're deliberately misunderstanding."

She had a point. But he didn't want to have this conversation. "Beth, you're tired and—"

"Don't do that." She jerked away, stepped back and stared, her eyes an intense shade of blue, her hair tousled in a way that made him think of scented sheets and bare skin. "I'm going to make it really easy for you, counselor. Tell me right now if you want to kiss me or not."

He inhaled sharply. Damn her, she knew the answer. If he lied, she'd know what a coward he was. He stared back for a moment, planning his strategy. His mind went blank. Without another thought, he reached for her, grabbed her arms a little roughly and pulled her against him, kissing her so hard he forced her head back.

Her gasp of surprise almost stopped him, but when she opened her mouth to him and touched her tongue to his lips, he dove in without a qualm. She tasted so damn sweet and her eagerness just about sent him over the edge. Except it was an untutored eagerness, a reminder of her lack of experience, and he forced himself to let up.

When he finally broke away, she gazed at him with anxious eyes. "Did I do it wrong?"

"What?" He was so damn hard he hoped his jeans hid some of his enthusiasm.

She lifted her shoulders in a timid shrug. "Tommy is the only boy I ever kissed. I mean really kissed. Not like fifth grade stuff." She briefly closed her eyes, her cheeks turning pink. "I shouldn't have said that."

David swallowed back an oath. She was right. He was confused. She baffled the hell out of him. One second she looked like a seductress, the next a child. It was clear he had to be the adult here, the responsible one who...

She moved up close and slid her arms around his waist, pressing her breasts against him, her belly, her thighs. His arousal hadn't gone entirely down. She had to feel it.

"Don't start thinking you've pushed me into anything again," she warned softly. "Believe me, I haven't been thinking about how to get away." She lowered her lashes. "I've been trying to come up with ways to seduce you. Obviously I'm not very good at it."

His arousal throbbed against her. His heart nearly pounded out of his chest. "Beth."

"Hmm?" She kissed the side of his neck where his pulse thundered.

He closed his eyes. He should stop her. Go for that walk and let them both cool off. But he couldn't move.

If he did, it would be to scoop her up and take her to bed.

"You're a good man, David," she whispered, her lips still against his skin. "I appreciate that fact that you don't want to take advantage of me. But this is my decision. My choice."

Good man? He sobered a little. "Don't fool yourself. I'm no Prince Charming. I've made my share of mistakes." He wondered what she'd say if he told her about Kathy. How he'd gotten her pregnant and stood by, self-absorbed and detached, while she miscarried.

"Everyone's made mistakes. God knows I have. But I know the man you are today."

Thinking back twenty years dampened his mood. "Don't be so sure."

She leaned back to look at him but she didn't break contact. Her hands rested at the sides of his waist. "I know what I've seen. How you helped me when you could have ignored the entire situation, and then even took me, a stranger, into your home." She put a finger to his lips when he opened his mouth to speak. "This is not about gratitude, got it?"

He didn't bother to nod, but waited for her to finish.

"You even changed a tire for that nice old couple. I bet you didn't expect to do that today, you softie."

That made him smile. No, he certainly hadn't expected to learn to change a tire.

She took both his hands and tugged him toward the bedroom. His heart lurched, and then they passed the bedroom door and disappointment set in when he realized she was actually leading him toward the couch.

Using her hands on his shoulders, she pushed him

down, and then surprised the hell out of him by curling up in his lap. She cocked her head to the side. "Now, what was I saying?"

He shifted, hoping she didn't feel the ready-to-erupt volcano down south.

"Oh, yes." She wiggled her bottom, apparently trying to get comfortable. Did she have any idea what she was doing to him? "Another thing is the terrific way you treat your mother and Ida. Do you know how much that alone tells me about you? I read about it in at least three different magazines. They can't all be wrong."

"Of course not." He inhaled the sweet scent of jasmine. Was it coming from her hair or her skin?

"And even when you're angry—and yes, I've seen you very angry, with Tommy for example." She shuddered and snuggled closer. "Even when you're angry you don't get out of control. You don't scream or yell or cuss. You just get really stern-looking, which is okay. When my brother Junior gets mad, the whole house shakes. I love him but that's not right. I know it scares his wife and kids."

She sighed. "Sorry, I didn't mean to get sidetracked."

"Better than embarrassing me."

"Am I?" She drew her head back, not looking apologetic but amused. "You shouldn't be embarrassed at all."

"Beth?"

Concern flickered in her eyes. "Yes?"

He put a hand on the side of her thigh, careful not

to let the touch become too intimate. "Do you have any idea what you're doing?"

Her throat worked as she swallowed. She was such a puzzle, major contradiction, a little naïve still, but bright and determined. Anyone who didn't sense her strength was a fool.

"Yes, I do," she finally said, and slid her hand between them, finding his straining erection.

Chapter Fourteen

Beth wondered when she'd gotten so darn brave. She wondered if David was aware her hand shook. He seemed pretty shaken himself so she doubted he knew how nervous she was, trying to act like she knew what the heck she was doing.

It wasn't that she had any qualms about making love with him, but she didn't want to disappoint, or just as bad, prove that she was young, naïve and inexperienced.

"Ah, Beth..." He took her face in his hands and kissed her gently at first. But then she rubbed him a little harder, his thick arousal hot against her palm, and he deepened the kiss, thrusting his tongue inside her mouth until she was breathless and so wet she would have died of embarrassment under any other circumstances.

But David's hands had moved to the muscles at her nape and he massaged and soothed, and she knew he'd never hurt or belittle her.

"Tell me what you want me to do," she whispered against his mouth, and was immediately sorry she said it when he retreated.

"Beth, this is no good."

"I only wanted to know how you like it." She had trouble meeting his eyes, worried that he'd see through her lie. As if her ineptness wasn't obvious enough.

He lifted her chin and gave her a sad smile. "I won't try and tell you I'm not turned on. I've been slightly transparent in that department," he said wryly, and that did make her smile a little. "But this is a big step and—"

"I know that." She clamped a hand around his wrist and lowered his hand from her chin. Then she leaned forward and kissed him again.

He let the kiss go on a long time before drawing back and saying, "Dammit. I'm trying to be noble here."

"Admirable." She kissed him again, hoping he'd take the lead. Soon. Before she ran out of bravado or pride. "Now, give it up."

His quiet laughter gave her hope, but when he slowly shook his head she was ready to throw in the towel. "You're making me insane, you know that?" he said, and then shocked her speechless by lifting her off the couch, into his arms and carrying her to the bedroom.

She clung to him, her heart pounding out of control, her palms starting to get clammy. How romantic was that? She swallowed hard, willing herself to calm down and not act like an inexperienced twit. Maybe if she just kept her mouth shut...

He laid her down on the bed, sat at the edge and brushed the hair away from her eyes. "We can stop at any time," he said, carefully keeping his gaze locked on hers.

"I know." She started to unbutton his shirt in case he had any notion of leaving her there alone.

He stopped her. "I'll be right back."

"Where are you going?"

"Just to the parlor." He kissed her. Hard. Forcing her to lie back on the pillows. He straightened, and the blatant hunger in his eyes sent a thrill down her spine. "I promise I'll be right back."

"Hurry."

He kissed her once more. Hard and fast, and then disappeared through the bedroom door.

She lay in the semidarkness trying to listen for any clues as to his doings. She thought she heard the rustle of paper and then the bathroom door close. Was he already putting on a condom? In a way, she hoped so. It would save her the embarrassment of fumbling with it.

Her new silk dress was getting horribly wrinkled and she thought about taking it off and slipping between the sheets. The idea of being so brazen as to let him find her naked when he returned was a bit unnerving. What if he'd changed his mind? What if he thought she was being too pushy? The spontaneity of being caught up in the heat of the moment was one thing, preplanning was quite another.

She sat up and rearranged the pillows, making sure when she lay back down she'd be at an angle that showed her best side. Her right cheek had a few less freckles than her left. Of course she'd taken special care to conceal most of them with makeup earlier.

Now, if she were naked, he probably wouldn't notice the freckles at all. There was something to be said for that side of the coin. Besides, a worldlier woman would probably think nothing of being naked and ready. Maybe he was more used to that kind of woman. Maybe a move like that would make her seem less young in his eyes.

She rearranged the pillows again. She wished he'd hurry before she drove herself crazy.

It seemed like an incredibly long time before she heard the bathroom door. Within seconds he returned to the bedroom, his clothes still intact. His gaze flickered down her body.

She tried not to stiffen. Had he expected her to be undressed already?

He set a couple of bottles of water he'd brought with him on the nightstand. "Had any second thoughts while I was gone?"

She'd barely given the first shake of her head when he'd reached for his shirt buttons. His eagerness made her heart flutter.

"Did you?" She watched, fascinated with each inch of smooth skin he revealed.

"Have second thoughts?" He laughed, more to himself. "At least ten of them."

She probably should be getting out of her dress at the same time, but she couldn't take her eyes off him. How had he found time to keep himself in such excellent shape? He wasn't heavily muscled or anything, but eye-catching ridges spanned his lean belly and he obviously did something to keep his chest in athletic condition. Except for a small splash of hair in the center, his skin was smooth and toned, stretching over just the right amount of well-defined muscles.

What was he going to think of her round, pouchy belly? She swore, even her thighs were a little flabbier now. And her rear end...

He threw his shirt aside and stepped out of his shoes. He never once took his eyes off her, and as thrilling and exciting the moment was, she wished like crazy she'd already gotten naked and was hidden beneath the sheets.

Instead of undoing his pants, he sat beside her again and worked some magic on her tense shoulders. "What are you thinking?"

"How good you look," she answered without hesitation.

He laughed. "I have a ruthless personal trainer come to my office three times a week." He massaged in silence for another few seconds as he studied her face. "What else are you thinking?"

She wrinkled her nose. "How round and flabby my tummy is, and how much I'd appreciate it if you turned the lamp off."

He looked surprised. He lowered his hand to cup her stomach. "It's not one bit flabby, and as far as round, small price to pay for a miracle, wouldn't you say?"

Unexpected tears burned the back of her eyes and she leaned forward and kissed him before he could see any sign of them. How different his reaction was from Tommy's. David considered the baby a miracle, not an unwanted burden.

She wished the baby were his.

Panic struck at the sudden thought and she retreated from him. She absolutely could not afford to be thinking such things. It wasn't right. The baby was her responsibility, and someday, she hoped, Tommy would recognize his son or daughter.

"Hey, what's the matter?"

She lowered her gaze when David tried to see her face. "I was just thinking how overdressed we are."

He didn't believe her. She saw the concern in his eyes, but bless him, he didn't push. He reached behind for her zipper, slowly disengaging it. Huddled in the safety of his arms, she put her hands on his bare chest and laid her cheek against his warm skin.

The dress slid off her shoulders and down to her waist. She felt him unfasten the back of her bra, and she held her breath. Slowly he drew away from her, and she started to panic, but then realized he only wanted to free her of the bra. He cast it aside and then gazed down at her bared breasts. Her nipples tightened and budded.

He cupped his hands beneath each breast, supporting their weight and rubbing the pad of his thumbs over her nipples. And then he lowered his head and kissed each one with such complete reverence she wanted to cry.

When he finally brought his head up, his eyes were slightly glazed. "You're perfect. Completely and utterly perfect."

"I'm not. I—"

He put a finger to her lips, and then replaced it with his mouth. With a little urging, she sank back against the pillows, and David managed to pull her dress off the rest of the way without breaking the kiss.

Finally they both came up for air, and he sank back and stared with unconcealed lust. No man had ever looked at her like that before and she was amazed she didn't have the urge to cover herself. He ran his hands over her breasts, and down her mounded belly, stopping to slide his fingers beneath the elastic of her bikini panties. She held her breath knowing he'd find her wetness. But he didn't hurry. Instead, he used his palms to outline her hips and thighs as though he wanted to touch every inch of her.

Beneath his fly his arousal grew thick and heavy and while she admired his restraint, she was getting a little impatient herself. But when she tried to reach for the snap on his jeans, he sat back out of reach.

Her gaze flew up to meet his.

He gave her a lopsided, boyish smile that made her heart constrict. "We might want to wait on that."

"I don't."

"Trust me. You do."

She swallowed. Dare she ask why?

He stretched out beside her, lying on his side, and cupping her cheek with his large gentle hand. "We don't want this to all be over before it starts."

"Oh."

He bowed his head to take a nipple into his mouth, and she closed her eyes and reveled in the feel of his wet tongue flicking the tight bud, laving, and then sucking until odd things started happening down south.

As he transferred his attention to the other breast,

his fingers dipped into her panties again. She sucked in a breath when he found her slick wet core, trying not to squirm under his skillful touch but she couldn't help it. He made a strange guttural sound and kissed her mouth, thrusting his tongue between her lips, his fingers repeating the action down below.

Beth grabbed his arm, not sure of she wanted him to stop or go faster. Heat threatened to inflame her and she couldn't form a single rational thought. She fumbled for his jeans' snap and managed to yank it free. The zipper wasn't so easy. But she was determined. She'd finally gotten it to move—and then she forgot about David as the sensations in her body surged. His fingers quickened, her muscles tensed. She cried out as she arched with such intense pleasure it took her breath away.

The delicious spasm ebbed when David moved his hand to her tummy, and she lay limp and confused and excited. Goose bumps crawled up her skin. David's kiss deepened. She closed her eyes tighter against the fireworks going off behind her lids.

What was happening to her?

Whatever it was, she didn't want it to stop.

"Beth?"

The voice seemed far away. The sensations had started to subside. She struggled to open her eyes.

"Sweetheart? Are you all right?"

Slowly she lifted her lashes to David's anxious face. "What happened?"

He looked confused for a second, and then worried, but then he smiled and kissed her briefly on her parted lips. "I believe you had an orgasm."

"Really? I thought so, but I wasn't sure."

His left brow went up but he said nothing, only brushed the hair off her damp cheek.

She couldn't believe she'd said that.

"Hey, what's that look for?" He touched the tip of her nose.

"I'm waiting for you to take off your jeans." It was only a small lie. Technically not even a real fib since there was truth in it.

His expression immediately changed. The lust was back in the slight flare of his nostrils, the darkening of his eyes. "Beth, we don't—"

She finished pulling his zipper down, extremely gratified at his sharp intake of breath. He tensed and then kind of slumped back.

She got up on one elbow and hoped she didn't make a total fool of herself. He must have sensed her hesitation, because he lifted his hips and helped her peel down his jeans, and then kicked them aside.

His boxers were black and silk and beneath them he was rock hard. Gingerly she ran a hand over his flat belly, and then cupped her palm over his thick shaft.

He stayed perfectly still, watching her through hooded eyes, but she could see the pulse at his neck going nuts. She took a deep breath and then slipped her fingers through the slit of his boxers and touched the smooth skin straining from his erection.

His eyes drifted closed and he groaned.

The sense of power that small reaction gave her fueled her curiosity and enthusiasm. She closed her hand around him, thrilling when it jumped in her palm.

"Ah, Beth, you have no idea—"

What she was doing? She quickly withdrew, afraid she'd totally blown it.

He brought her hand back. "You have no idea how good you make me feel."

A soft, nervous laugh escaped her.

"Come here." He urged her down to meet his mouth. His kiss was sweet and tender.

Nice, but she wanted more. She slid her tongue across the seam of his lips.

He groaned again. A moment later he got up, pulled off his boxers and ripped open a foil packet he took off the nightstand. Fascinated, she watched him sheathe himself.

When he looked up and their gazes met, heat raced through her body. Heaven help her, the fireworks were about to start again.

IT WAS STILL DARK when Beth awoke. All she could see was the red glow of the digital clock. At some point she remembered vaguely turning off the lamp. She didn't need light to know David was beside her.

His arm was still around her as he slept, and she snuggled closer still, her cheek pressed to his chest, as she listened to his heartbeat.

Even with touching him it was hard to believe they were here together, that they'd made love. Twice. That he'd used endearments and told her she was beautiful. And without any reservations, she believed him.

David was incredibly gentle and tender, yet his skillful hands and mouth had nearly sent her over the brink. Heck, he *had* sent her over the edge. Who knew a body could do and feel those things?

She sighed softly, knowing she had to get up and go to the bathroom. He stirred a little when she lightly kissed his stubbled cheek, and she froze until she felt she could slip away without waking him.

Hoping not to disturb him, she skipped the bathroom attached to the bedroom and went out to the parlor. Still naked, she glanced at herself in the mirror over the wet bar. The light was dim, but not enough to hide the imperfections, like the two small dimples on her left thigh, or the bulge of her tummy that frankly had been there before she got pregnant, and still, she'd never felt more beautiful.

She made her way to the bathroom and closed the door before she flipped on the light. On the counter was the package David had returned with when he'd disappeared earlier. Small and flat, she supposed there could have been condoms in there at one time, but it looked an awful lot like it contained a book.

A book? How strange.

She forgot all about using the john, and peered down at the white paper hoping she could see through it. No luck.

Did she dare out-and-out peek?

Unethical, yes, but if she wanted to get another moment's sleep tonight…

Taking a deep breath, she carefully slid her hand inside and pulled out a book. Nothing else was in the sack. She looked at the title. *Pregnancy And Birth Book.* Two pages were marked with store book-markers—sex in pregnancy and being an involved father.

She closed the toilet lid and sank down. If she hadn't already fallen in love with David, she'd be hopelessly head over heels now.

Chapter Fifteen

David stared at his open day planner and played with the paper clips he'd pulled off the Henderson case brief. He'd started reading the damn thing two times and had to stop because his concentration was so poor his retention was almost zero percent.

Four days since they'd returned from Napa and he'd gotten almost no work done. What the hell was wrong with him? Other than he thought about Beth *all* the time. Even though they'd mutually decided to cool things in front of his mother, he'd bet his Jag she knew something was up. In fact, he suspected she might even be trying to keep them apart.

Only once had he had the opportunity to be alone with Beth in the house, and lo and behold, his mother came barging into his study just as he and Beth had started to get cozy.

Another thing that bothered him was that Beth hadn't seemed well the past couple of days. He'd tried to get her to see a doctor but she claimed the symptoms were a normal aspect of the pregnancy. That didn't stop him from feeling guilty as hell. Not just for last Saturday night but because he couldn't wait to get her naked again.

His phone rang but he ignored it, letting his secretary pick up the call. If his private line had rung, he would have snatched it up in a hurry. Not that Beth ever called him. But just in case...

A knock at his open door made him look up. His secretary had a grim look on her face. "It's Mr. Gretzky's office. You missed another luncheon appointment with him."

David blinked, stunned that he'd done it again. Twice in two days. What the hell was wrong with him?

"Do you want to talk to him?" Cassie asked. "He's pretty angry."

"Of course I will." David picked up the receiver and pressed the button to get connected. "Harrison, how are you?"

He winced when the man answered with a violent curse. The guy was obviously over the top furious. David had never heard that kind of language come out of his biggest client's mouth.

"How the hell do you think I am, Matthews? I waited for you at the St. Francis for two hours." Harrison cursed again. "I'm glad your firm is doing so damn well you can afford to piss away my business."

David did some mental cursing himself, and then loosened his tie. "Come on, Harrison. How long have we known each other? Don't I get a chance to explain?"

"Go ahead. Explain why you wasted four hours of my time these past two days."

Excellent question. David massaged his left temple. He doubted the man would understand that a certain blue-eyed blonde had consumed all of David's thoughts. "Something personal came up. You know this isn't like me, Harrison. Give me two days to get with Johnson and Holmes. They've been working full-time on your defense strategy."

"Two days, Matthews, and if I don't approve of your approach, I'm hiring a new firm." He slammed the phone in David's ear.

The guy was bluffing. He'd been a client for three decades. He'd started his multimillion-dollar electronics business about the same time David's dad had started the law firm. The two men had been more than client and attorney. They'd become friends over time. Surely, Harrison would cut David some slack.

He stared at the stack of pink messages of unreturned calls. But why should he? Why should Harrison or any client be faced with the decision to change firms because David had screwed up? Because David hadn't been doing his job. His father had to be turning over in his grave.

David sat back in his chair and rubbed his tired eyes. The truth was, he had shamefully neglected his work. Not just for the past two days but for over a week. He'd been leaving the office early, not taking work home with him. Or when he had, his briefcase remained closed.

He pressed the intercom to summon Johnson and Holmes, the two attorneys assigned to Harrison's company's defense against a lawsuit that had been filed for a faulty security system. The case was a no-brainer, there was no chance in hell they'd lose, but Harrison deserved his full attention.

The last thing David needed was to lose his father's oldest client. Wouldn't that just be great? How better than to prove David was the same screwup he'd always been?

"So far I think everyone we've invited can come to the party." Maude checked another name off the list. "Except for Prudence Merriwether. She and her latest boy toy will still be in Europe. I don't know what she finds to talk to him about. Honestly, after an hour, what do you do with a boy less than half your age?"

Beth smiled and continued to cross-check her list against the caterers' invoice. She was used to Maude's bluntness by now, and she actually admired the older woman's broad-minded view of life. Although she occasionally made comments about her friends' states of affair, Maude never judged or expressed disapproval.

So why hadn't David told his mother about them?

The thought sometimes nagged at Beth. Was David ashamed of her? Did he regard their night together as a one-time fling and unnecessary to mention?

No, that couldn't be the case. He wasn't like that. If anything, he was probably ashamed of himself, not her. Which was ridiculous. She'd gone willingly to him. Heck, she'd practically forced herself on him.

The problem very likely was inside her head, a product of wayward hormones. She'd been feeling crummy lately, suffering from bouts of morning sickness she'd smugly thought she'd avoided until now. On top of that, she hadn't had an opportunity to be alone with David, which meant her imagination was in overdrive, speculating on what he was thinking, what he was feeling…how he'd changed his mind about them.

She'd lost count of how many times she'd replayed their ride back. How he'd managed to touch her the entire return trip to San Francisco, kissing her at stop signs, even pulling over about a half hour from the house for some last-minute smooching.

But after they'd pulled into the garage, it was business as usual. Although she knew he was incredibly busy at work, Beth was having a heck of a time not taking the distance that appeared to exist between them personally.

"You've been good and sneaky, Beth," Maude said. "And don't think I don't appreciate it."

"Excuse me?" Beth bolted out of her preoccupation and stared at the older woman.

"I don't think he suspects a thing, do you?" The amusement in Maude's watchful eyes made Beth wonder how much *Maude* suspected.

She'd made a couple of other comments earlier that had Beth thinking the older woman might be fishing. Not that Beth had given her any hints. In fact, to some degree, Beth had been guilty of avoiding David. Except for that time in his den, and then they almost got caught.

"No." Beth shook her head. "He's been awfully busy at work. I doubt he's even thought about his birthday."

"I hope so. He's informed me half a dozen times he does not like surprises. I don't want him getting any fancy ideas about heading for the Caribbean or Hawaii.''

Beth froze with her pen in midair. She hated ambushing him, and she certainly didn't want him angry with her.

''Don't worry.'' Maude smiled. ''Once the festivities are in full swing, he'll be glad he has all his friends here to help him celebrate.''

Beth sincerely hoped Maude was right. She stood and gathered their teacups and leftover shortbread cookies. ''Well, I'd better start dinner.''

''Oh, didn't I tell you? I'm meeting Marjorie Carrington for dinner at the club.''

''Oh.''

''I'm sorry. By all means make yourself something or order takeout. As far as David is concerned, I wouldn't worry about preparing anything for him.''

Beth barely heard what Maude was saying. All she could think about was being alone with David tonight. Of course she'd make something special for dinner to go along with one of the wines he'd bought in Napa, and then she'd take a long moisturizing bubble bath, then do her hair, maybe put it up in one of those more sophisticated styles she'd found in *Cosmo* yesterday.

Maude glanced at the grandfather clock sitting in the corner of the library. ''Oh, my, I'd better start getting ready. Marjorie wants to have cocktails first.''

Beth felt only a tad guilty that she couldn't wait for Maude to leave the room. As soon as she did, Beth forgot about the tea things and hurriedly gathered up her paperwork so that she could start cooking and primping.

Two hours later, the mushroom and wild rice stuffed Cornish game hens were in the oven, the crispy skin turning golden brown, while a bottle of sauvignon blanc chilled in the fridge. She'd already washed and dried her hair but hadn't decided on which of two styles to attempt.

Another hour later, she'd turned off the oven and sat near the window watching for David. Her hair had turned out great and she'd even managed to get two coats of coral polish on her fingernails. She glanced at the clock, and then checked the answering machine again in case he'd left a message while she was in the bathroom.

Nothing.

She covered the Cornish game hens with foil and stuck them in the refrigerator, and then she resumed her post by the window, huddling on the sill cushion, praying he wouldn't be much longer.

At ten-thirty, she gave up and went to bed.

PLANS FOR the party ran smoothly for the rest of the week. God knew Beth had plenty of time to even out any rough edges. David worked late every night, usually coming home after she'd gotten in bed.

She tried not to take it personally. After all, he'd explained that an upcoming trial had him in a time crunch and having taken the weekend off to go to Napa Valley had put him behind schedule. She understood that, but still she couldn't shake the sick feeling that distance was growing between them.

Three days before the party, he chose to come home early. Beth was on the phone with the caterers when he entered the library. Luckily, she caught him out of the corner of her eye.

"I can't wait to see you," she said suddenly to the confused woman on the other end of the line. "I never thought I'd miss Rock Falls so much. Have the leaves all turned color already?"

"Ms. Anderson, I don't understand—are you all right?" The woman sounded so flabbergasted, Beth had to bite her lower lip to keep from laughing.

"I'm terrific. How's your sister? Will she be there Saturday morning?"

The woman remained silent for a long moment, and then she asked, "By any chance, is the birthday boy listening?"

"Absolutely." Beth kept her back to the door, but she sensed David hadn't left.

"Yes, my assistant will be there early Saturday morning ahead of the truck. She'll go over the setup with you before the men get there with the chairs and tables and such."

"Excellent." Beth was going to have to call the woman back. She was no good at all this cryptic stuff.

"Now, we have the matter of two or three bartenders. You weren't sure how many you wanted the last time we spoke."

"Oh, yes." Beth paused. "I think I'll leave that up to you. I'm totally flexible."

"How about one outside on the patio and one inside at the wet bar in the living room. That should suffice since you'll have a sommelier handling the wine."

"Perfect. I look forward to seeing him, too."

"Ms. Anderson, maybe we ought to talk later." The woman chuckled. "When the walls don't have ears."

"Good idea."

"Don't worry. Everything will turn out well."

"I hope so. Talk to you later." Beth hung up, and took a deep breath before turning around.

David stood in the doorway, the oddest look on his face. Oh, God, had he heard something he shouldn't have? Did he know about the party?

"Hi." He didn't smile, and he looked horribly tired. Just like he had all week.

"You're home early." She tried to sound normal, but it wasn't easy. If she'd given anything away about the party, Maude would strangle her.

"Early?" He studied her for a long uncomfortable moment. "It's after seven."

"Early for you these days." It came out a little curt, which obviously didn't escape his notice.

His expression tightened. "This is a busy time for the firm. We have several trials coming up next month."

She sighed. "I didn't mean to sound ugly." She moved closer, hoping he'd meet her halfway. "I miss you."

He stayed in the doorway. "Where's Mother?"

"She's in her room on the phone. Ida called about a half hour ago and they've been talking ever since."

David glanced at the red light on the library phone signaling Maude's line was still in use. The coast was obviously clear. Beth moistened her lips in anticipation, anxious to feel his arms around her, his mouth on hers.

He didn't make a move to approach her. "I brought home some work. I'll be in my study."

"David?"

He'd already started to leave but he stopped, taking a moment before he looked at her.

"Is something wrong?" She clasped her hands together so he couldn't see how nervous she was suddenly.

He opened his mouth to say something, but then closed it and shook his head.

"David, you're not being fair."

"Look, work is piling up. I'm tired." He pushed an agitated hand through his hair. "That's all."

"I don't believe you," she said softly, surprised at herself. Normally she avoided confrontation in any form.

His left brow went up. "I'm sorry if you're feeling neglected." That was all he said and then turned to leave again. End of discussion for him.

Beth swallowed hard. Why was he behaving like this?

Her thoughts flitted back to last weekend, how he'd barely been able to keep his hands off her on the trip home. She remembered the book he'd bought on pregnancy, how he'd urged her to see a doctor. What had happened to that man?

"David?"

This time it looked as though he wouldn't stop. But he did, his reluctance evident in the stiff way he turned to face her.

"Would you like me to bring you some dinner into your study? I made salmon and pasta."

His expression softened for an instant. "Maybe later."

Her heart lightened. "Just let me know. I'll be in here writing a letter."

A sudden frown pulled his brows together. "Maybe you ought to think about a trip home before you start showing."

Beth blinked. Where had that come from? "Are you trying to get rid of me?" she asked, teasing, holding her breath, nervous that that was exactly what he was doing.

His smile was sad. "Just figured you might be homesick."

On impulse, she hurried over to him, put her arms around his neck and kissed him, looking for reassurance.

God, but she wished she'd found it.

DAVID TRIED to concentrate. It was useless. He glanced at the clock. Ten-fifteen. He wondered if Beth had gone to bed yet. He hoped so. He didn't think he could face her again. Not with the hurt in her eyes, or the way she wrung her hands together.

Granted, it had been a tough week and he knew he'd disappointed her on a couple of occasions by not showing up for dinner, but dammit, he had a firm to run. Not just any firm, but one of the most prominent in the city, thanks to his father's hard work and vision. The very least David could do was maintain Matthews and Matthews' reputation.

He scrubbed his face, and then laid his head back on the chair and stared at the ceiling. What a mess.

He didn't blame Beth for wanting to go see her friends back home. He just wished she'd been honest with him.

A woman that age needed excitement, not just to hang around the house all day. He understood that. Did she think she owed him now that they'd made love? Or had she made love to him because she'd already felt she owed him?

He let out a frustrated breath. He had no business dwelling on Beth. That's what had gotten him into these predicaments with both Gretzky and Andrew Clemons. Gretzky was still ticked, and picking apart every defense strategy the team offered. David could see it was going to take a while to soothe his ruffled feathers.

A knock at the door had him straightening in his seat. He glanced at the checkbook lying open on his desk, and then closed it. A check for cash was already half made out.

Before he could answer, his mother came in with a disapproving frown on her freshly washed face. Without her usual makeup, she looked drawn and tired. "What? You can't come out and be social anymore?"

"Hello to you, too, Mother."

"My point exactly." She sat in the chair opposite him, arranging her voluminous purple silk caftan around her legs. "What's been the matter with you these past few days?"

"I've been working."

She studied him closely like she used to do when he was a kid and she grilled him about why he'd missed his curfew. "I ran into Barbara Gretzky yesterday."

Great. "We're working on a case for Harrison," he said needlessly. No doubt Barbara had already given his mother an earful about David's ineptness.

"I heard the old windbag is giving you a hard time." His mother chuckled. "Don't let him get to you. He used to rake your father over the coals every once in a while."

David frowned. He couldn't picture anyone messing with his formidable father. Not only had he been a damn good attorney, but he hadn't been the type of person people questioned. "Hard to imagine."

"Why?"

"I don't now. Father always seemed to be right, I guess." He thought back to his first year in college. "I remember the day he'd lost his one and only case. You would've thought another earthquake had hit San Francisco."

"Oh, yes, I remember it as if it were yesterday. What a spectacle he'd made of himself, shooting his mouth off to anyone who would listen."

David stared at her, surprised. He didn't remember the incident that way at all. The jury had clearly been wrong. Even the newspaper reports indicated the defense had been sandbagged.

Her mouth twisted in a wry smile. "To say your father was not a gracious loser would be quite an understatement."

"But he shouldn't have lost that one."

"Perhaps. But the argument could be made he shouldn't have won some of the ones he did."

David had to be more exhausted than he thought. He couldn't believe his mother was saying these things. Everyone had always idolized David Matthews, senior. Including his wife.

She snorted. "Don't look at me that way. I loved him dearly but your father was more fallible than you realized. But enough about him. Tell me, did you have an argument with Beth?"

"No. Why?"

"Because she looks as though she's been crying half the evening."

He stiffened. Damn, he'd upset her. "Maybe she's ill. Did you ask her? She's looked a little pale lately."

"Glad to see you're at least concerned."

"Of course I am. Where is she now?"

"In her room, but if you didn't upset her, I can't imagine what you can do to help." A shrewd glint in his mother's eyes said she knew more than she'd admitted.

He opened the checkbook to the check he'd partially written and turned it to face his mother. "This is for Beth. I think she's been homesick. This will pay for a first-class plane ticket and accommodations once she gets there." He looked up to find his mother gaping at him, stunned disbelief in her face. "Why are you looking at me like that?"

"You've got to be kidding."

He clenched his jaw and returned her stare.

"Do you want to break that poor girl's heart?"

He laughed without humor. "By giving her an all-expense paid trip home?"

"I know you aren't that stupid, David. God help me I didn't raise you to be a damn fool."

"What are you talking about?"

"How can you be so insensitive? You must realize Beth is in love with you."

Love? His chest tightened. His laugh came out rusty. "You're joking."

"I'll tell you something else," she said, studying him intently. "I think you feel the same way."

"That's absurd." He threw down the pen he'd been fiddling with. "How can you say that? I hardly know her."

"Your father and I got married a month to the day we met."

"Now you're talking about marriage?"

She smiled. "Not exactly."

"The whole idea is preposterous. After I give Beth this money and she's back home with her friends and family, I bet the most we hear from her is via a letter or two."

Anger flashed in his mother's face. "You are not offering her that money."

"She keeps telling me she's not a child. Let her decide what she wants to do with it."

Her anger faded into sadness and disappointment. "Don't do it, David, don't be like him. Don't try and pay her off."

David searched for something to say, his concern growing by the second. He wondered when her last checkup had been. She was making no sense, and it scared the hell out of him. "Relax, Mother, this is only a gift. Beth will understand."

She shook her head and slowly got up. "You always wanted to be like your father. Congratulations. You are indeed his son."

"What are you talking about?"

"When things get rough or people become a little inconvenient, you just pay them off."

"Mother, you'd better sit back down."

She laughed. "I don't need to sit down, I need to get out of here before I say something I regret."

"Frankly, you aren't making much sense, and I'd like to call Dr. Helms."

"Ah, David." She put a hand to her throat, and a million worst-case scenarios shot through his head. "You accuse Beth of being naïve. But you get the grand prize." She paused, her face creased with misgiving. "Kathy didn't have a miscarriage."

"Kathy?" Why would his mother suddenly bring up the past? They hadn't heard from or spoken of his old girlfriend in eighteen years. God, he hoped this wasn't a sign of early dementia. "Kathy did miscarry, but why are you bring this up now?" he asked gently.

She gave a sad shake of her head. "No, that's what your father wanted you to think. The truth is, he paid her to have an abortion so she and the baby wouldn't ruin your career."

Chapter Sixteen

David sat back down, stunned and confused. Denial was so strong, morosely half of him hoped his mother was suffering from some form of dementia. The alternative was just too incredible.

"How do you know this?" he finally asked when he thought his voice wouldn't fail him.

"He told me. I begged him not to make the offer without consulting with you. But you know your father…he knew best for everyone."

David still wasn't sure he believed her. "Why didn't you tell me before now?"

"For God's sake, David, I couldn't tell you at the time. You and your father had had enough of a rocky relationship. And then later, it seemed rather pointless."

"How do you know Kathy took the money?"

"I was there." She looked away. "I was totally against the entire deal, but I couldn't stand up to your father. Not then, and not that it would have done any good. He wouldn't have backed down. Certainly not for me."

At the sadness in her voice, David winced. This wasn't a dream or figment of her imagination.

"Please understand." She reached across the desk for his hand. "Your father and I had a lot of good times, but he wasn't the easiest person to live with, and I accepted that. I simply don't want you to have this image of him on a pedestal. He was far from perfect, and I pray someday you'll stop trying to live up to his unreasonable expectations."

David squeezed her hand. That was all he could offer for now. He had a lot to think about and he wanted to do it alone. "You look tired. Why don't you go on up to bed?"

She hesitated. "Beth does love you, you know. I can see it in her eyes every time she looks at you. Be careful, son. Don't hurt her. Or yourself."

He waited in silence for her to leave the room and close the door behind her. Damn, if he didn't feel as if he'd been dragged over five miles of rough road. How could his father have done such an underhanded, despicable thing?

And Kathy, too—maybe he hadn't been as emotionally available as he should have, but he'd promised to take care of her and the baby. She'd had an obligation to tell him she wanted to abort their child.

Anger and hurt and resentment swirled inside his head. For years he'd felt guilty about the miscarriage. He'd been wild and irresponsible and rebellious, and he'd blamed himself for causing Kathy too much stress.

He cursed out loud.

All that wasted emotion for nothing.

Damn his father.

David closed his eyes and laid his head back. And then there was Beth. Sweet, trusting Beth. Subconsciously was he really trying to pay her off? He honestly didn't think so. If anything, his ego smarted. On the phone earlier, she'd sounded so eager to see her friends.

In fact, it seemed she might have already planned the trip but had left him out of the loop. Just like Kathy.

He put the brakes on. The two situations couldn't be compared. Nor should the two women. What Kathy had done was in a league by itself. Beth only wanted to be among friends, and who could blame her? He certainly hadn't been around for her.

Just like he'd been unavailable to Kathy.

There was no way of getting around it. Even in his ignorance, he'd been a major player in the outcome nearly two decades ago.

He brought his head up and massaged the back of his tension filled neck. Too many thoughts and recriminations warred between his temples. He'd do best to put the information out of his head for now. Right now his mind was like an open wound, the least thought or memory a major irritant.

What he needed was a stiff drink, maybe two. And then at least attempt to get a good night's sleep. There was nothing he could do about the past, but he sure could screw up with Beth if he weren't careful.

His gaze fell on the check he'd started writing. He picked it up and tore it in half. If helping her to get on with her life turned out to be the best thing to do, he could always write another one later.

If he'd learned nothing else in thirty-nine years it was that when he didn't know what to do, he was better off doing nothing. And right now, he'd never been more confused in his life.

IF BETH hadn't had the party preparations to keep her busy, she would've lost her mind. The planets had to be misaligned or something. Maude suddenly doubted the wisdom of having the party, and although David still seemed preoccupied, he'd become more solicitous and present. While that was nice and reassuring, she didn't need him in her face while she was trying to keep his birthday bash a surprise.

Boy, would she be glad when it was all over. And when it was, a few things were going to change around here. She and David were going to have a frank talk. Maude knew something was going on between them, Beth was fairly certain, and she was miserable trying to pretend the mere sound of David's voice didn't send her heart soaring.

How could she have fallen for him so quickly? Especially after her experience with Tommy. Was she that insecure? That needy? She'd thought a lot about that for the past ten days. But she knew deep in her heart that her feelings for David had to do with the man himself, and nothing more. He made her smile, he made her laugh, and he never once made her feel ashamed of the pregnancy. If anything he seemed anxious, constantly asking how she felt and if the baby was behaving.

Beth put a pot of coffee on to brew before she went to check on the progress in the library. Only the trim was left and the painter promised he'd be done today after she'd nearly threatened him with bodily damage. The party was tomorrow evening and the chatty man was two days behind schedule.

Panic started to simmer and she forced herself to calm down. Think good thoughts. Everything else was going smoothly. David was going to be really surprised. Pleasantly, she hoped.

She stopped in the foyer to sniff a rose from the bouquet on the console table, and smiled thinking about yesterday when David had tentatively asked if he could feel her tummy. Of course it was too soon for him to feel anything, but she'd happily granted his request. Cupping his palm over the soft mound, he'd kissed her, briefly, sweetly.

And then disappeared for the rest of the evening.

Sighing, she continued on to the library and froze at the door. "What are you doing?"

The small weathered man looked up from the magazine he was reading. "Taking a break."

"You just had one half an hour ago. I brought you cookies and tea."

He shrugged. "My neck was getting a little stiff."

Beth's patience snapped. The man had been late every day, took long lunches, talked her ear off every time she entered the room, complained about every ailment known to man and had finally admitted he was filling in for his son, who was the person originally recommended to her.

She folded her arms across her chest. "Than I suggest you take some aspirin and get back to work."

Mr. Sanchez's eyes got wide and he immediately closed the magazine.

"You will recall that you promised to have the job completed two days ago. I believe I've been relatively patient. You will have this room finished today, won't you?"

He sprang to his feet. "Yes, ma'am."

"Thank you." She turned to leave.

David was just outside the door.

She put a hand to her chest. "You scared the hell out of me."

His eyebrows shot up in surprise...probably because he'd never heard that language out of her before. Heck, she'd used the word twice just this week. Rare for her.

"Sorry, I was just on my way to the study."

"What are you doing home so early?" Her thoughts scrambled back to her conversation with Mr. Sanchez. Had she mentioned the party? God, she hoped not. No, she didn't think she had.

"I'm meeting a client out here for a drink. We have an upcoming trial to discuss." His gaze went past her toward the library, a hint of amusement on his face. "How's everything coming?"

"Fine. Today's the day. Everything will be completed and back to normal."

The corners of his mouth twitched. "I'm sure you're right."

She made a face. "You heard."

He cupped her cheek and stared into her eyes until

her knees grew weak. "Don't ever apologize for being assertive. You handled him very well."

Her breath caught. Not because of his words, but the way he still looked at her. As if he wanted to scoop her up and carry her into his bedroom. If he did, she wouldn't utter a peep.

He lowered his hand. "I'd better get going or I'll be late."

She swallowed her disappointment. "Do you know what time you'll be home?"

"Not too late, I hope, but don't wait dinner for me." He hesitated, started to say something, but then turned and headed down the hall.

She watched him until he disappeared. Would she ever grow tired of looking at him? She doubted it. He had more than a nice body and handsome face, he had character in the lines at the corner of his eyes, and kindness and understanding in his heart. She honestly didn't know a better man.

She took another peek in the library and was pleased to see Mr. Sanchez busy working. She was about to return to the kitchen to start dinner, when she remembered she'd taken a phone message for David.

The information was on the kitchen counter and she grabbed it before heading toward David's study. His door was open but she knocked anyway. He didn't answer so she peeked inside. His chair was backed away from his desk as if he'd recently gotten up. Surely he couldn't have left that quickly.

She hesitated for a moment, debating if she should leave the message on his desk. Finally she decided that would be best. She crossed the room and out of the corner of her eye, noticed movement in the attached bathroom.

She stopped and started to back up, not wanting to embarrass David or herself. But then she saw him leaning toward the mirror, studying his hair. His fingers sifted through the area above his left temple, the only place where there was a slight sprinkling of gray. He frowned, and then checked the other side.

He wouldn't find any gray there. She knew almost every inch of him by now. The thought made her smile. So did the way David straightened suddenly, turned to the side and sucked in his already flat belly.

She pressed her lips together to keep from making any noise and slowly backed toward the door. Of course it wasn't funny. God only knew how she'd react to turning forty...or thirty, for that matter.

She sighed to herself. Poor David. She hoped Saturday would be his best birthday ever.

THIS HAD TO BE the worst day of his life.

David stared at the sea of both familiar and strange faces in his living room.

"Surprise! Surprise! Surprise...!"

A friggin' chorus assaulted him before he could even close the door behind him.

"Happy birthday, darling." His mother rushed forward and kissed both his cheeks. "You're home early. I'm afraid all the guests haven't arrived yet.

Great. He forced a smile for the crowd of what had to be a thousand people already. Okay, maybe fifty people. But one person more than his mother and Beth would have been too many. He scanned the room for her. She was in the back corner watching him, a shyness in her expression that tugged at his heart.

He cleared his throat. ''Well, this is quite a surprise.''

''More like a shock, judging by the look on your face,'' said Marjorie, an old friend of his mother's.

Several people laughed.

''This wouldn't happen to be the big four-o, would it?'' Parker King asked with a wicked grin, causing more laughter.

David cringed. ''Let's see, Parker, you have at least two or three years on me, right?''

His friend chuckled. ''That doesn't bother me a bit. It's the wife and three kids who make me nuts,'' he said, and then grunted when his wife, Sandy, elbowed him in the ribs.

Everyone seemed to have a crack to make and by the time a waiter brought David a glass of champagne, he was more than ready to down half the bottle. It appeared everyone had already been imbibing and sampling the hors d'oeuvres being passed by white-gloved waiters before he'd arrived. Good. The sooner everyone was done and gone the better.

For now he'd be pleasant and gracious. Later, he'd wring his mother's conniving neck. And Beth...how much had she to do with all this?

She'd disappeared from the corner and he wandered toward the kitchen looking for her, stopping to make the dreaded small talk, and take the occasional ribbing. Outside on the patio he saw the tables and chairs set up, and he cursed to himself. Dinner was obviously part of the program. This was going to be one hell of a long night.

Beth wasn't in the kitchen. The caterers had pretty much taken over so he migrated toward the dining room. No Beth there either, but a couple of young ladies were talking and laughing with one of the waiters.

"Hi, Mr. Matthews, happy birthday," the blonde said when she saw him. She smiled, flashing impish dimples. "I bet you don't remember me."

Mr. Matthews? Jeez, she couldn't be much younger than Beth. He studied her a moment. She did look familiar, but he couldn't place her. "I'm afraid you've got me stumped."

"Stacy." Her grin widened. "Bill Conroy's daughter.

"Little Stacy?" His college roommate's kid? David nearly let out a most inappropriate word.

She laughed. "I'm not that little anymore."

No, she wasn't. Holy sh—!

"My dad's wandering around somewhere. He wants to challenge you to a game of one-on-one basketball. But I wouldn't worry. He's gotten a little paunchy in his old age."

David choked. The guy was only two years older than David. "I'll be sure to not tell him you said that."

"That's okay. I tease him all the time." She giggled, and then brought a flute of champagne to her lips.

He narrowed his gaze. "How old are you?"

"Nineteen, and Dad said I could have one glass."

"Well, all right." God, he even sounded old. "Enjoy the party."

"You, too. Oh, Mr. Matthews? Cool music."

He listened a moment, but he didn't recognize a single bar. Only that it was that current variety, which if played any louder would give him a headache.

He sighed and headed toward the patio, his mood plummeting. If Kathy had had their child, he or she would be about that same age as Stacy by now. Amazing. Depressing.

He grabbed a second flute of champagne, briefly thinking he should substitute scotch instead. The quicker he reached oblivion, the better. But then he caught a glimpse of Beth near the pool and all other thoughts fled.

She had on a becoming yellow dress and her hair was up in some sort of sophisticated twist. Taupe-colored high heels helped show off her nicely shaped legs. She looked stunning and he couldn't wait to tell her.

In fact, he wished everyone would go home so he could tell her in private, and watch the color blossom in her cheeks. He loved the way she blushed at the least little thing, and then that would make her mad and the color would deepen and her eyes would turn the most remarkable shade of blue.

He'd been thinking a lot about what his mother had said, but he still wasn't convinced Beth was in love with him. She'd been in serious trouble, and he'd rescued her to some degree. Of course she was grateful, and it would be easy to confuse gratitude and security for love.

Although he had to admit, Beth was a lot stronger than he'd initially given her credit for. She was strong-willed and had enough self-confidence to get out of the relationship with Snyder.

Maybe David still wasn't giving her enough credit. Maybe she knew her own mind. Maybe he was the only idiot who didn't know what he wanted. No, he knew what he wanted. He wanted Beth, but life was more complicated than giving in to selfish desires.

His memory started to drift to the past, to his father, to disappointment. He stopped cold. His mother and Beth had gone to a lot of trouble to arrange the party. He wasn't pleased with the whole thing but he wouldn't be a jerk about it. Thinking about the past was bound to sour his mood even more.

If he concentrated on Beth, everything would be all right. Everyone would eventually go home and tonight he would take her to his bed. In the unlikely event his mother had a problem with that, she'd just have to get over it.

For a moment he lost sight of Beth, and he ducked his head to see where she'd gone. But she'd disappeared. He opened the sliding glass door to the patio, but before he made it outside he glimpsed someone approaching rather hurriedly from the living room.

It was Tom Snyder.

Chapter Seventeen

"What are you doing here?"

Snyder stopped cold, his megawatt grin fading. His gaze darted toward a couple talking and sampling skewers of bacon-wrapped shrimp near the patio door.

David was relatively sure they hadn't heard him, but that didn't excuse his rudeness. He swept a glance in the last direction he saw Beth, relieved there was no sign of her.

Obviously Snyder had been invited. Just as the other attorneys from the firm had been, David realized, cursing to himself for his stupid oversight. His mother couldn't have known about Snyder's relationship to Beth.

"Come with me," he told Snyder, and quickly led him to the den before the guy saw Beth. Or she saw him. Assuming she didn't already know he was here.

He closed the door behind them.

"I was invited," Tom said before David could say anything more. Anger simmered in the younger man's eyes, but he kept his cool.

David didn't ask him to sit. "Of course you were. I apologize." The words nearly stuck in David's throat, but better that than Tom finding out Beth was here. "I was simply surprised to see you."

"Meaning I shouldn't have come." Some of the charm and composure slipped. "I thought we'd already buried the hatchet over my *personal* problems."

David motioned to the chair opposite his desk. There would be no easy way to end this conversation. The hostility in the younger man's face and voice sealed that verdict. Rotten timing, but if laying the cards on the table meant keeping Snyder away from Beth, then so be it.

"I'm going to get to the point." David took his seat behind the desk. "I want you to find another job."

Snyder's head drew back in surprise, unchecked anger darkening his face. "That bitch contacted you again?"

David barely hung on to his own fury. "Any number of firms would be eager to acquire a man with your qualifications, and of course, I'll give you a glowing recommendation."

"What did she say?"

"Beth has said nothing more about you." David stared Snyder in the eyes, ignoring the terseness of his tone or the resentment in his face. "I'll use any connections I have to get you a comparable position at an equal or better salary."

"You can't just fire me." Snyder stood, his right fist clenching. "My job performance has been impeccable."

"In exchange for your resignation, I'm also prepared to offer you a generous…an extremely generous severance package." The flicker of interest in Snyder's eyes made David sick even while he counted on the man's greed. "However, I have two conditions that must be met—you have no more contact with Beth, and you give up all rights to the baby."

"You can't do this."

"I'm merely making an offer." David leaned back in his chair and watched the tug-of-war on Snyder's face. Pride versus avarice. Hard to tell which was winning…anger maintained a foothold through it all.

"You bastard," Snyder finally said, and David didn't so much as blink. "Who the hell do you think you are interfering in our business?"

David smiled. "Her lawyer."

The door opened, and Beth stood in the doorway, looking from him to Snyder. She seemed angry. No telling how long she'd been standing there with the door ajar, or how much she'd overheard.

Beth's entry was soundless but David's expression obviously gave something away. Snyder frowned and turned around. "Beth?"

She stayed focused on David. "Your mother is looking for you," she said calmly, and then she glanced at Snyder. "Hello, Tom."

"What are you doing here?" He shook his head, looking confused, dazed, and then glared at David. "You invited her to your party?"

Looking eerily serene, she said to David, "Thank you for speaking on my behalf, but it really isn't necessary." And then she turned to Snyder and smiled.

His mouth curved in a cocky grin and he held his arms open to her.

David's heart sank. How could she still have feelings for the jerk?

But she didn't go to him. She glared at Snyder, her smile turning cynical, until he lowered his arms, his expression turning to one of disbelief.

"What are you doing here?" she asked, her voice perfectly calm.

Snyder snorted and gave David a caustic look. "I was invited."

Beth's expression wavered then, her uncertain gaze flickering to David.

"Mother handled the guess list, I assume," he said, and she nodded. "I didn't find it necessary to give her any details. Obviously, had she understood the situation…" He looked at Snyder. "You wouldn't have been invited. Under the circumstances, I think it best you leave."

"What the hell is going on here?" Snyder looked from David to Beth, outrage and disbelief pinching his features. "You two shacking up together?"

"Tom," Beth said quietly in spite of the color flooding her face. "Grow up."

"Beth." He put a hand out to her.

She moved aside. "Leave, Tommy, there's nothing here for you."

He lowered his arm, his hand beginning to fist. "The hell you say." His insolent gaze went to her belly. "In three months I'll have plenty of reason to be in your face."

Her abrupt laughter sounded giddy. "Five months, but of course you weren't listening. You don't care about the child. Can't you just leave us alone?"

"Yes, I do care." His eyes glinted with mockery. "It's mine."

"Listen, Snyder..." Unable to stand it a moment longer, David ignored the hand Beth put up to him. "If you so much as—"

"David!"

The sharpness in her voice got his attention. And silence.

"I can handle this," she said, keeping her focus on Snyder. "Besides, Tom doesn't want to cause any trouble, do you?" Before he could reply, she added, "Of course I'm no lawyer, but you using my credit card without my permission is considered illegal, right?"

Snyder muttered a curse.

She smiled. "Not that I plan on pressing charges. Unless I have to."

Anger distorted Snyder's features. "I'm still the kid's father. Don't piss me off, Beth, or you might find that the road can get pretty rocky."

David opened his mouth to blast Snyder, but Beth gave David a stern, silencing look.

"I don't think that'll be a problem," she said quietly. "After all, I doubt you want this mess dragged out when you start your new job. Traipsing in and out of court in front of your new colleagues would have to be embarrassing. And believe me, tick me off and that courtroom had better have a revolving door."

Snyder stared at her in stunned silence, and then skewered David with an accusing look.

"This has nothing to do with him, Tom." She waited until she had his full attention. "We had a long history, so I put up with more than I should have. But I won't be your doormat.''

Snyder glared a moment longer, threw a final hostile glance at David, and then stormed out the door.

David barely paid the guy any attention. He stared in awe at Beth. Her hand shook slightly as she tucked back a stray tendril of hair, but she seemed fairly composed. He'd already seen evidence of her strength and assertiveness, but the way she handled Snyder, not once backing down was really something.

"You're incredible. I'm so proud of you." He reached for her hand, but she moved out of his grasp.

"And you," she said, her eyes narrowing. "What gives you the right to speak for me?"

David blinked. She looked pretty angry. "I wasn't really—I was trying to help.''

"Hadn't I asked you to stay out of it? That I would deal with Tommy?''

"Yeah, but—''

"But you think I'm too young and naïve to handle my own affairs.''

"I didn't say that.'' Panic stirred in his chest as her expression turned to saddened resignation. He had no defense. He knew she didn't want his interference. Isn't that why he hadn't admitted to his first conversation with Snyder?

The despair in her eyes burned a whole in his gut. "You're never going to see me as a woman, an equal, are you?''

"That is absolutely not true.''

"You think you need to take care of me. Even when I don't want that.'' She shook her head and laughed, the sound bleak. He wanted to cut in, but he gave her the floor. "Do you want to know the real irony? I've grown up in the past couple of months. I know what I want out of life. I want a partner who's my equal."

She moved closer and lifted a hand to cup his cheek, and he relaxed under her touch. "So David, I really wish *you'd* grow up."

Giving him a brief, sad smile, she lowered her hand and then disappeared before he knew what had happened.

He stared at the closed door for a moment, stunned, annoyance seeding. By the time he went after her, she'd disappeared into the crowd.

SHORTLY AFTER ten-thirty, Beth slipped into her room and locked the door. Dinner had been over for two hours, and the caterers no longer needed any direction from her. Maude readily bought the excuse that Beth needed to get off her feet. Too readily. She had a feeling the older woman had noticed how Beth had been dodging her son all night. Not that he seemed all that anxious to talk to her.

She kicked off her shoes and sank onto the soft queen-size mattress. Her dress would wrinkle like crazy but she didn't care. She lay back, rested a hand on her nervous tummy, and stared at the ceiling.

The encounter with Tommy still had her a little shaky. How she managed to talk to him without babbling or stuttering like an idiot, she had no clue. No, that wasn't true. She had a good idea why she'd kept her wits about her. She'd been so focused on David that Tommy seemed insignificant.

Overhearing the way David had taken control of her problems, of her life had really struck a raw nerve. A fact she hadn't wanted to face was now too glaring to deny. He would always see her as someone young and vulnerable, someone needing his protection, and not as an equal.

She'd made mistakes and she'd surely make more, but they were hers to make and learn from. Maybe a year ago Beth could have lived like her sister-in-law did, having Junior make all the decisions, smoothing any bumps in the road his own way.

But Beth wasn't willing to give up her independence. She wouldn't be foolish. After all, she had a baby coming. But she needed some distance from David. It wouldn't do her or the baby any good to fall more deeply in love with him. Not until he shook any lingering paternal feelings. If that were even possible.

The thought of breaking away made her sick to her stomach. She hated being separated from him during a normal workday, much less an indefinite period. But what did she have, really? His smile, his nice words, his financial support…all those things were wonderful and for which she was truly grateful. But emotional support was what she craved, and a healthy respect for her need to be independent.

Her gaze flew to her closed door. Was that a knock? Listening carefully, she heard the light knock again, and then David's voice calling her name. She closed her eyes and lay perfectly still, as if that would prevent him from seeing the lamplight seeping out beneath the door.

She couldn't talk to him now. She had to think, and

she was much too exhausted to trust herself to be rational. He called her name again, and she turned over onto her side, her back to the door. A few moments later, he left Beth in welcomed silence. Now if she could only get rid of the doubt screaming in her head.

"I CAN'T SAY forty agrees with you." Maude lumbered into the kitchen, looking drawn and tired as she slid David a curious glance on her way to the coffeemaker. "You look like hell."

"Good. It suits my mood."

She poured herself a cup of the strong brew, and then sat across from him at the table. "What are you doing up so early?"

"I couldn't sleep." He noticed the darkness under her eyes. "What about you? This is a little early, isn't it?"

"I couldn't sleep either."

David eyed her as she sipped her coffee. Weariness lined her face. Planning the party, staying awake until the last guest had left, had to be tiring for her. "Have I thanked you for the nice party?"

She smiled. "You hated it."

"What I hate is turning forty." He stared down at the cup, his mood too dark to pretend he was anything but totally miserable.

"Guess what? Forty isn't the end of the world. Some people think life gets better."

"So I've heard."

"Frankly, I'm surprised age is an issue." She paused, reaching across the table to give his hand a pat. "What's really bothering you?"

"As if you didn't know." He slumped back and met her concerned gaze. "Have you seen Beth this morning?"

"Briefly."

He waited for her to elaborate, perhaps tell him what an ass he'd been. To his amazement, she said nothing. "Beth's angry with me and she has every right to be."

His mother's eyebrows shot up but still she said nothing.

"I've been treating her like a child."

A smile tugged at her lips, but when she didn't comment, he thought twice about confiding anything more. It wasn't as if she could help. He knew what the problem was, and what he had to do to solve it. At least he thought he did...

He drummed his fingers on the table and let his gaze stray out the window toward the bay. Through the scattering of gray clouds he could see the top of the Golden Gate Bridge, tempting him to get in his Jag and head into the city and the safety of his office. There he could bury himself in work and block the disquieting awareness that had kept him awake all night.

But that would be the coward's way.

"The thing is," he began slowly, "I don't think of her as a child at all. That's the main problem."

He paused for a reaction. A look. A word. Anything. Although known for often offering more opinions than he cared to hear, his mother sipped her coffee and patiently waited for him to continue. He muttered a curse, which did get a reaction.

Her face creased in disapproval. "Honestly, David, look who's acting like a child."

"That's the point. I've been behaving like an idiot and I might have blown it with Beth."

"What happened?" Oddly, she didn't look surprised or even that curious.

A red flag went up as David studied his mother. She wasn't normally one to guard her expression. But she did now. Beth had already talked to her.

"David? Tell me what's bothering you."

"What's Beth told you?"

She gave him a patient smile. "Does it matter?"

Hell, yeah, it mattered. He briefly closed his eyes. His mother was right. He had nothing to lose. "I've been treating her like a child to put distance between us. To remind myself that she deserves someone closer to her own age, someone she has more in common with…someone who could give her more children."

His mother laughed. "For goodness sakes, you act as if you're eighty years old. Anyway, Beth can speak for herself."

"Yeah." He thought about Tom Snyder. "That's another part of the problem. I stuck my nose in her business when I shouldn't have."

"Well, what's the bottom line?"

David frowned at his mother's abruptness. Exhaustion chased away the last of his patience. "What do you think? I love her."

She calmly nodded. "Then I suggest you go tell her. She's packing and she's already called a cab."

"Packing?" His gut clenched in a painful vise. He

pushed back from the table, nearly toppling the chair over as he got to his feet. "She can't do that."

"I wouldn't bet your Jag on it."

He spun around at the sound of Beth's voice. She stood at the kitchen door, arms crossed, her face expressionless.

How much had she heard? It didn't matter. "Beth, you can't run off without giving me another chance."

"Why not?"

"Because it's against your nature, your sense of fairness. Because you..." He cleared his throat. "Because I—"

"Excuse me, I think I hear a faucet dripping somewhere." His mother gathered her voluminous lavender caftan and hurried out of the kitchen.

Beth's gaze held his. "You were saying."

He took a deep breath. "I love you."

She blinked, her arms falling to her sides. "When and how did you arrive at this conclusion?"

"Last night." He moved closer. "Actually, I've known for a while, but I finally admitted it to myself, staring at the ceiling all night and wondering what my life would be like without you."

"Your life was fine without me."

"Fine isn't good enough anymore." He took one of her limp hands and kissed the back of it. "I want you to make me laugh and second-guess myself. I want to feel you in my arms every night when we go to sleep. I want to help you raise this baby," he said, cupping his hand over her belly.

She caught her lower lip with her teeth. "What about our age difference?"

"I promise not to treat you like a child, and you promise never to buy me a cane. Unless, of course, I ask for one."

Her lips twitched with threat of a smile. But the sadness that lingered in her eyes made him uneasy. "It's not that simple."

He shook his head. "No, it's not, but I kept thinking about that couple who own the nut shop. Remember them?"

She nodded, her expression cautious.

"He's got to be at least fifteen years older than she is, and at one time they likely had a similar discussion. He probably worried about getting old and becoming a burden to her, and she would hear nothing of it. I bet they never counted on the reverse happening."

The corners of her mouth began to lift.

"And you know what?" He tugged her toward him. "I would be willing to bet the Jag he doesn't consider her a burden in the least."

"I think that would be a pretty safe bet." She gave him a beautiful smile full of hope.

"For better or for worse, in sickness and in health. Isn't that the way it goes?"

"I think so," she said with searching eyes.

"Marry me, Beth. I promise you all those things and more."

She gasped. "But—"

"Love never means having to say 'but'." He grinned at the comical face she made. "And I do love you."

"Okay, you can have your way." She smiled as her lips headed for his. "This time."

Epilogue

"Don't forget my overnight bag." Beth put a soothing hand to her belly as another contraction threatened.

"Right." David turned around and went back into their room. Three seconds later he returned empty-handed. "Where did I put it?"

"In my closet."

"Right."

Beth smiled in spite of the fact she was ready to explode. Her polished, composed husband, who could be a pit bull in the courtroom, was a mess. The closer she'd gotten to her due date, the jumpier he'd gotten.

"Ready?" He had the wrong bag.

"Honey, I need the blue one."

"Damn, I'll be right back."

She sighed. He had many good qualities, but being an expectant father had him undone.

His hair was uncombed and his shirt untucked. She'd barely said his name and he'd rolled out of bed and grabbed the car keys. "This is it, right?"

"That's it," she said as he took her elbow. "Did you tell your mom or Ida we're leaving?"

"I'll call them later."

"But—"

"Mommy, Daddy, where are you going?" Two-and-a-half-year-old Lindsey plodded out of her room, rubbing her eyes.

"That's why you have to tell them now." Beth smiled at her daughter. "Honey, Mommy and Daddy have to go to the hospital now."

David crouched down and drew their daughter between his spread thighs. "Hey, sleepyhead." He brushed the blond hair away from her face. "Remember how we told you that we would be getting you a little sister soon?"

Lindsey yawned and nodded.

"That's what we're going to do right now. So how about you get back in bed? Nana will stay home with you. She'll come see you soon."

"Okay, Daddy." She kissed his cheek and stumbled back into her room.

David immediately stood. "Okay, I'll go tell, Mother."

Beth watched him hurry down the hall. He'd been the best father to Lindsey, adopting her right after she was born. And as far as a husband, Beth couldn't have designed one better herself, but if he didn't hurry and get her to the hospital, she was going to clobber him.

She stiffened with another contraction, took deep breaths and counted to ten. She opened her eyes in time to slide her arms around David's neck as he scooped her up into his arms. He'd always be her hero.

HARLEQUIN®

AMERICAN *Romance*®

**Coming this July from
national bestselling author**

Judy Christenberry

**a brand-new story in the
Brides for Brothers series**

RANDALL HONOR

The Randalls are a family of deep bonds and
unquestioning loyalty. But Victoria Randall has
never felt as if she was really part of this wild
Wyoming clan. Then she meets the town's
handsome new doctor and sets off on the
adventure of a lifetime…learning what true love
and honor are all about!

And be sure to watch for more Randall stories
coming from Harlequin Books, including a very
special single title, **UNBREAKABLE BONDS**,
available this August.

Available wherever Harlequin books are sold.

HARLEQUIN®
*M*akes any time special®

HARLEQUIN®

AMERICAN *Romance*®

invites you to meet the citizens
of Harmony, Arizona,
with a brand-new miniseries by

Sharon Swan

A little town with lots of surprises!

Don't miss any of these heartwarming tales:

HOME-GROWN HUSBAND
June 2002

HUSBANDS, HUSBANDS...EVERYWHERE!
September 2002

And look for more titles in 2003!

*Available wherever
Harlequin books are sold.*

HARLEQUIN®
Makes any time special®

Visit us at www.eHarlequin.com

HARWTH

Princes...Princesses...
London Castles...New York Mansions...
To live the life of a royal!

In 2002, Harlequin Books lets you escape to a world of royalty with these royally themed titles:

Temptation:
January 2002—*A Prince of a Guy* (#861)
February 2002—*A Noble Pursuit* (#865)

American Romance:
The Carradignes: American Royalty (Editorially linked series)
March 2002—*The Improperly Pregnant Princess* (#913)
April 2002—*The Unlawfully Wedded Princess* (#917)
May 2002—*The Simply Scandalous Princess* (#921)
November 2002—*The Inconveniently Engaged Prince* (#945)

Intrigue:
The Carradignes: A Royal Mystery (Editorially linked series)
June 2002—*The Duke's Covert Mission* (#666)

Chicago Confidential
September 2002—*Prince Under Cover* (#678)

The Crown Affair
October 2002—*Royal Target* (#682)
November 2002—*Royal Ransom* (#686)
December 2002—*Royal Pursuit* (#690)

Harlequin Romance:
June 2002—*His Majesty's Marriage* (#3703)
July 2002—*The Prince's Proposal* (#3709)

Harlequin Presents:
August 2002—*Society Weddings* (#2268)
September 2002—*The Prince's Pleasure* (#2274)

Duets:
September 2002—*Once Upon a Tiara/Henry Ever After* (#83)
October 2002—*Natalia's Story/Andrea's Story* (#85)

Celebrate a year of royalty with Harlequin Books!

Available at your favorite retail outlet.

HARLEQUIN®
Makes any time special ®

Visit us at www.eHarlequin.com

HSROY02

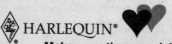

Brides of the
DESERT ROSE